The Hostage Bargain

Reading order

The Hostage Bargain

The Wrong Idea

The Deeper Game

The Most Wanted

The Hard Way

The Best Trick

The Hostage Bargain

THE BANK ROBBERS BOOK 1

ANNIKA MARTIN

Chapter One

I WAS LOOKING SUPER BUSY AT MY FIRST CITY National Bank teller window one day, which means I was scowling at Facebook like it was a very important spreadsheet. Now and then I'd hit random keys on my adding machine.

That's when the three bank robbers burst in.

They wore zombie masks and yelled lots of loud commands all at once, like they were really angry. One of them smashed a glass display kiosk with his gun, and it made a loud crash.

My jaw dropped. My heart pounded. Instinct told me to stay very still...but I also really wanted to get a video of it.

But then one of them said, "Put your hands where we can see them!" And he was growly enough that I put down my phone and raised my hands.

In addition to the masks, they wore business suits and leather gloves, and they moved with military precision. There were only three of them, but it seemed like they were everywhere with the way they took the place over.

Customers and co-workers cowered. People cried. These were my people, my neighbors, and I had this urge to get in front of them and protect them. I so didn't want anybody hurt!

But at the same time, I secretly approved of the way these robbers were trashing the bank, because any enemy of First City National Bank was a friend of mine. A BFF bestie.

Hank Vernon and his evil bank had destroyed my family. Relentlessly, cruelly, methodically destroyed us.

So, yeah.

One of the robbers broke another glass thing and then he looked at me like he wanted me to be scared.

All I could think was, *Dude, you are acting out my deepest fantasy. Break more stuff! Please!*

He glared at me hard, all green eyes and menacing movements, but I wasn't scared...I was turned on.

Did he know it?

They commanded all seven of us tellers to keep our hands up —so we wouldn't push any silent alarm or panic buttons, I guess.

What they didn't know was every single one of us tellers at First City National Bank of Baylortown, Wisconsin hated bank owner Hank Vernon with a passion—a seething, lava-like passion churning deep in our bank teller hearts.

Any one of us would've loved to see his bank go down in flames, hopefully taking all of the greedy, predatory Vernon family with it.

I was the queen of the Bring-Down-Hank-Vernon Brigade, being that I had more Vernon-inflicted wounds than all of my co-workers put together.

The green-eyed robber ordered the other tellers to throw down their phones and march around to join the customers on the floor, but he pointed at me and said, "You! All the money. In the sack."

I nodded, taking the sack from him, wondering how I could get the maximum amount of Hank's money into it, and also, *in the sack*? Was he being humorously suggestive?

"Touch anything else and you're dead," he said.

"Don't worry, dude. I'll do whatever you want."

His gaze intensified. Excitement shivered across my skin.

Did that sound sexy?

Yes, it sounded sexy.

It was official: a zombie-mask-wearing bank robber and I were having a moment.

Adrenaline pumped through my veins, one of my favorite feelings in the world. It reminded me of being on top of a ski jump. That delicious point where you take off and you're careening out of control.

He gestured at the sack with his gun, and I started grabbing money.

More yelling out on the floor. "Down! Fingers knit or I blow your heads off!" As if to emphasize his point, one of the robbers kicked the coin-counting machine over onto a glass table, creating an earsplitting crash. Somebody whimpered. I frowned. These poor people didn't deserve to be frightened.

"Send us off with tracking devices or exploding dye and you're dead," my guy growled at me. "We'll come back and mess you up." Then he grabbed the flowers out of the little vase at my station, ripped them up, and threw them on the floor.

Okay, then!

I moved to the next drawer. "I'm telling you, don't worry. I'm into it. Tell Scary Spice out there not to shoot anyone and we're good."

His green eyes blazed. Was the '80s reference a little too obscure? "I make the rules here. Not you," he growled.

My belly tightened; that was a little bit hot, the way he said it. Did he know? Was he being hot on purpose?

"Ten-four," I said, finishing the job, cleaning out drawer after drawer.

My breath sped as I gave him back the bag. His leather glove brushed against my bare skin and his eyes locked on mine. I had this feeling that he was looking right through me, that he *recog-*

nized me. Not personally—I'd have known those green eyes anywhere—but like he knew how excited I felt.

And I really, really liked the feel of his glove on my skin.

This robbery was working for me!

Years ago, my mom showed me an article that talked about how thrill-seeking people like me are missing a brain chemical, and that we make up for it by taking risks. She showed it to me hoping I'd stop taking so many risks, but all the article did was make me feel glad to be missing the brain chemical. I can't imagine going through life without leaping from the cliff over Mucklanaho River, or racing down the abandoned ski slide, or getting excited about green-eyed criminals with their competence porn commands and sexy gloves.

"The safe." His gaze glowed behind his mask. "Who can get us in?"

"Oh, I think you'll be pleasantly surprised," I said. "It's open." Hank had left for the day, and the rest of us weren't exactly conscientious when he was gone.

"Thor!" He waved his gun at one of the other two robbers.

A guy in a blue zombie mask jumped over the counter with startling athletic grace and said, "Three minutes twenty."

"*Thor*? As in the Norse god?" I asked.

That pair of green eyes bored fiercely into mine.

Gulp.

"Lead us back."

I turned and led them back, straight into the walk-in vault, and pulled open the money safe. My big, green-eyed robber ripped the camera from the wall and tossed it to the floor like it was nothing. Then he pulled bundles of money off the shelves with fast, efficient movements while Thor held the bag. These men had done this before. It was so badass. My stranger sex fantasies would never be the same.

"Three-five." Thor pressed a finger to his headset.

"What?" the big green-eyed one asked.

"Nothing. Traffic," he said, probably listening to the police scanner.

Suddenly I came to my senses. I was missing a couple major destroy-Hank-Vernon opportunities here.

I caught Thor's eye. I held up a hand—*stop*—and put my finger to my lips—*shhh*— then I pointed to the listening device on the shelf. Hank planted it there to catch employee grumbling, but we all knew about it.

"Zeus." Thor pointed to it.

Zeus.

"Please don't shoot me," I warbled in my best fake-scared voice. "Please." I pointed to a section of bills—fifties. I ripped off the seal, displaying the trackers for them to see, and I pointed to all the bundles that had trackers. They had little red marks, and we were supposed to leave them there in case of a robbery. I felt like a lady on the shopping channel demonstrating the features of a new product. If they had a shopping channel for badass robbers in zombie masks who named themselves after gods.

Thor and Zeus exchanged glances. I expected them to throw the trackers onto the ground, but my green-eyed Zeus pocketed them. Clever. He was getting sexier by the second. I also liked that these guys had named themselves after gods. It demonstrated confidence.

And I had something more to show them.

The Vernons had started investing in gemstones as a hedge against the economy. Hank and his sister had recently acquired a collection of loose diamonds at an auction. They were supposed to bring them to one of the branches with safety deposit boxes, but if there was one thing you could count on, it was Hank's laziness. My gaze fell on the strongbox shoved way back on the floor. Could the stones still be in there?

I hesitated—if I showed them the diamonds out of the blue,

the Vernons would know I'd gone out of my way to help the robbers. Yet, I so wanted the robbers to have them. This was the Vernons' private property and wouldn't be FDIC insured.

I cleared my throat and, imitating a man best I could, I barked, "What else is in here?" The two of them looked at me like I'd lost it. I winked. Then, in my regular voice, I said, "What do you mean what else? There's nothing else!" I knelt and pulled out the strong-box, opened it. A mound of velvet bags sat inside.

Yes! The diamonds. Still there.

I let out a cry. "Ow! Please! What more do you want? What do you want from me?" Of course they weren't hurting me, I just wanted it to sound that way for the recording. No doubt I seemed like I had a split personality, one half threatening the other, but hey, you don't get that many chances to screw the Vernons.

I yanked out one of the bags. Zeus gestured with his gun, and I emptied it into my hand, then looked up in mock surprise. *Diamonds.*

Thor eyed Zeus, then turned to me and said, "You show us everything there is to see now, or we'll kill you! Now! Everything!"

I nodded. Thor was into it.

Zeus pocketed the diamonds while Thor yelled at me some more. "What's in that box? You fuckin' show me!"

"I don't want to die," I said in my most weepy way. I felt like part of the gang.

They grabbed up every last diamond.

Thor stiffened as he put his finger to his ear. "Suspicious activity, this address."

The third robber burst in. "Guy out there dropped a dime."

"Fuck," Zeus said.

I felt it was a bit petty to worry about a dime; had they not just gotten money and diamonds?

Then I realized it was slang for *made a phone call.*

Also, I realized the three of them were looking at me.

It was like they'd all gotten the same inspiration at the same time, or a group communication from the mothership.

"We don't take hostages," Zeus said.

What? Hostages?

"No choice," the scary third one said.

"Agreed." Roughly, Thor grabbed my arm.

Hostages? Shit! I tried to think of what happened to hostages in various movies I'd seen, if they usually got killed or not. Then I remembered—*they're movies.* Anyway, I was on their side. Surely they understood that.

"Odin!" Zeus threw one bag to the scary robber, then another.

Odin. Another god.

Thor grabbed my arm and put a gun to my head, and we ran out of the safe and down the back hall; they seemed to know the layout as well as I did.

The gun freaked me out. "You don't have to be so...you know..."

"Yes, I do," Thor said as we burst out the door. He practically dragged me across the parking lot.

Odin had something in his hand, like a video game controller. He punched a button, and just like that, an earth-shaking boom ripped through the air.

Flames blazed from a car in the parking lot.

Another explosion came from the other side of the lot. Flashes. Smoke gushed into the air from all directions.

"Hey!" I said. "Be careful—that bank's full of innocent people!"

"Nobody's getting hurt," Thor said, pushing me along. "Just some fireworks."

I nodded, feeling a little sad that they thought exploding cars were fireworks. Had their parents never taken them to Fourth of July celebrations?

Under the cover of smoke, we headed into the alley, toward a white van with *Romano's Catering* emblazoned on the side. Romano's was an actual restaurant a few towns over, but I doubted these guys were from Romano's.

Somebody slid a door open. Thor pulled me into the back seat. "Eyes shut! Now!" he commanded.

I shut my eyes. Doors were slammed and we were off. I heard something that sounded like fabric ripping.

"I'm going to blindfold you," he said softly. Five little words that had me blushing. How was he doing this to me? "We can't have you seeing our faces, or we'll have to kill you."

I nodded obediently. I told myself I should be scared, but it still felt thrilling.

It wasn't about sex. I assumed that Odin and Zeus were up front and had probably taken off their masks. Two men in zombie masks driving a van didn't exactly project the image of innocence they were likely going for.

Still.

Sirens sounded. I braced, eyes shut, as the van peeled out and turned.

"It's okay," Thor reassured me, knotting the cloth at the back of my head without getting any of my hair caught, a skill that impressed me.

For somebody who didn't typically take hostages, he was pretty handy with a blindfold.

"None of us want to kill anyone," he continued. "So let's stay strangers. We'll let you off once we know we won't need you, got it?"

"Got it."

"Hands."

I put out my hands and he bound my wrists with efficient movements...for a bandit unused to hostage taking. The sirens grew louder, cranking the air of tension inside the van. Where were we?

"Fuck," somebody said.

Were the sirens for us?

The sirens passed.

"Okay, then," Thor mumbled.

Whichever robber was driving—Zeus or Odin—he was driving sanely, which pleased me. I figured the biggest danger would come with a high-speed chase at this point.

Train-crossing bells.

I felt the van slow. Low voices up front. I could feel the rumble through the seat.

"Are we held up by a train?" I asked loudly.

A door creaked open. What was happening? Had somebody bailed from the van?

"Because if we are," I continued, "there's a bridge you can take."

"You think we're idiots?" Odin barked; I could tell it was him because I knew that Zeus had a deep voice, and Thor was right next to me. Also, Odin had just a hint of an accent. "I think we know the logistics of the area," Odin added.

"Just trying to be helpful."

"Don't be," Odin said. "We are awesome at this, and we don't need your fucking input." Odin's accent involved saying the "g" just a little bit too hard, so it sounded like *your fucking ginput.*

A door slammed and we squealed out—a U-turn from the feel of it.

Softly, Thor said, "We needed to get rid of those trackers."

"Did you throw them into a train boxcar?" I asked.

No answer.

"Very clever. Kudos."

Somebody up front grumbled. Maybe kudos isn't the thing you say to bank robbers who have taken you hostage.

"I want you to know something," I announced. "I won't be any trouble. My main mission in life is to screw the owner of that bank. And I'm not talking sex. Even if I saw your faces, which I swear I haven't, I would never tell. I want you to get away." When nobody replied, I said, "I'm on Team Bank Robbers." Still no reply. "Just so you know."

"Can you shut her up?" Odin grumbled. He got into a hushed conversation with Zeus in the front.

"Fine," I whispered.

"Don't worry about him," Thor said to me. "We'll find a place to let you out and you'll have your fifteen minutes of fame." I felt the seat depress next to me—Thor, sliding closer. He lowered his voice to a hushed, sexy tone. "We have to find the right sort of place, though. There's an art to every part of this."

I nodded. There was something so delicious about his familiar tone, like he was confiding something sexy.

I couldn't see their faces, but I was starting to differentiate them by personality as well as voice. Thor was smart and easy to get along with, and we seemed to be on a certain wavelength. He was the one who'd immediately understood why I was talking in different voices in the safe and then played along.

Zeus was the big silent green-eyed robber who oozed masculine hotness.

Odin was the one who'd seemed the craziest during the robbery. A bad-boy techie with an accent and a high opinion of their bank robber prowess. The three of them seemed sane and even kind of cool, yet excitingly dangerous, being that they were bank robbers. The combo was working for them.

Sirens in the distance. "Oh, no!" I said.

"It's fine," Zeus said. I imagined him there in the front, his green eyes and solid presence, utterly in control of everything. I wished I could see what he looked like. I wished I could see all of their faces.

Chapter Two

THOR SAID, "WHY DON'T YOU TELL ME WHY YOU HATE your boss so much."

I rested my head back on the seat, trying to think where to start.

"That bad, huh?" Thor said.

"If it wasn't for Hank Vernon, my parents would still be alive," I said.

The hush in the car deepened, like they all really took that in.

"I'm sorry," Thor said softly.

"It's been five years," I said. "I'm..." *Getting used to it* wasn't quite right. More like struggling to live with it. "I'm okay."

"What happened?" Thor asked softly. "What did he do?"

I told all about how Hank Vernon and his family wanted to take our sheep farm away from us. They wanted to run us off the land and lease it to a company that mined frack sand because they'd make way more money than they would make off of the mortgage their bank held.

I told my bank robbers about how amazing my mom and dad had been, standing so strong against the Vernons. Like scruffy warriors, my folks. That farm had been their life.

I took a breath. "Right after I graduated from high school, we had a fire in one of the barns and missed some payments, and that let Hank Vernon change the mortgage terms. He doubled the payments. We got so behind; we were in so much debt."

My parents needed a bunch of money fast, so they signed on for a two-month gig on a fishing boat in Alaska. The money from it would get us caught up. Lambing season had ended, and my three younger sisters and I were old enough to run the place over summer.

I swallowed, remembering the last time I saw my mom and dad. "Two weeks in, the boat went down. They were killed. Just... gone." It's still hard to tell it. To relive the shock.

"I'm sorry," Thor said.

"Thanks," I said. Such a small word for how much I missed them. "There was a bit of insurance money that let us catch up, but..."

"Your parents were gone."

"Right," I whispered.

"What happened to the farm?"

"I kept it up. I managed," I said.

Back before all that, my plan had been to leave Wisconsin to start my life—I had this whole round-the-world bungee jumping and rock-climbing trek dreamed up. I was going to pick up odd jobs along the way and maybe finish college somewhere with mountains, or at least near a ski jump.

Once they died, I was all about caring for my sisters and keeping the farm.

Not letting the Vernons win.

I tried not to think of the life I'd planned before the Alaskan boat accident. The secret truth is that I'd always wanted to escape the farm. Now it was impossible.

Thor said, "Bungee jumping is pretty dangerous, you know."

"So are guns."

Thor laughed softly. "I'm impressed you managed to keep the farm. Good for you."

"We expanded our cheese-making operations and started making these awesome wool comforters that we sell online," I said.

"So why are you working at his bank?" Thor asked. "If you hate him so much?"

"I'm buying time. There's a balloon payment coming up that we'll never be able to handle. Hank said it could be delayed if I worked at the bank. But you know—wink wink—he thinks I'll do some extracurricular work duties. Which I've avoided because, let's just say, *no way*."

"I'm glad we hit his bank," Thor said.

"Oh, me too." I grinned. I couldn't remember the last time somebody fought for me. That's how it felt. "Did you notice how nobody pulled the silent alarm? Everyone there hates him."

"Wouldn't've worked anyway," Odin said from the front. "We took it out."

"Maybe I'll buy a Paris Hilton quilt," Thor said.

"Oh, please do!" I smiled in his direction. Nicest. Bank Robber. Ever! "May I suggest the organic Paris Hilton Deluxe comforter?"

"Yeah?"

I snorted. "I'm just kidding. That one costs twenty thousand dollars. It's kind of a pie-in-the-sky product that we made to cheer ourselves up. Like, *hey, maybe Paris would buy it*. Or the Kardashians. Our normal comforters are a few hundred bucks. They're very well made."

"Hey, you exchanging phone numbers back there or what?" Odin grated. "Can it."

Wistfully, I pictured nights sitting around the kitchen table with my sisters, freaking out over the latest vet bill or whatever. Times like those, one of us would say, *"It's okay because Paris Hilton will be buying these comforters for every room in her house soon, including one for her dog. Isn't that great?"* It was our favorite inside sister joke.

"Would you say that's true of all FCN banks?" Zeus asked. "Do all of the employees want to bring down this Vernon guy?"

"Not as much as the branches he actually visits. They have 132 branches across the Midwest, dude. Vernon can't terrorize them all. Hey, you know what would be awesome?" I fumbled for Thor's arm and clutched it. "If you gave me one of those diamonds. That could go a long way toward helping us protect the farm. I could pay the entire balloon with one of those!"

Thor laughed softly. "I don't think so."

"What's so funny? I showed you where they were. I could have it cut up and fenced or whatever. Isn't that what you guys'll do?"

"But the difference is that you would never get away with it, and we will," Thor said.

"You think I can't figure it out?"

"Nope," Thor said.

"What? Just nope?"

"That's right, *nope*," he said. "'Cause we've got skills, baby."

"You've got *skillz*."

"Amazing skills like you've never seen."

My belly went tight. Was Thor as focused and confident in bed as he was in robbery mode? I'd never know. These guys were unlike any other guys I'd ever met. And in the area of competence porn? Off the charts! Even in zombie masks.

I said, "Are you truly unable to impart these skills?"

Thor lowered his voice to a silky rumble. I couldn't see his eyes, but I felt like all of his attention was focused on me. "We don't impart them to just anybody."

"Because your skills are so very god-like?"

He shifted in the seat next to me. "Very," he whispered.

I blushed. "And you would never impart them to a common mortal like me?"

Was I flirting with this guy?

Yes!

I'd be back to my regular life tonight. I loved caring for my sisters and the farm, but I sometimes felt so trapped. And here was this moment in time where I'd been plucked out, whisked away.

And I already had a blindfold on...

"And why would we do that?" he breathed into my ear. "Why would we ever, *ever* do such a thing? What would persuade us?"

The subject was no longer diamonds—that was clear. "Perhaps you will impart your skills because you are benevolent gods," I said.

"Well, we *can* be benevolent, it's true. Benevolent beyond your wildest dreams. But we can also become quite wrathful."

Heat speared my core. What was happening to me?

Somebody in the front cleared his throat. Warningly.

Thor seemed to straighten up. Were Zeus and Odin the bosses of him?

Either way, I straightened up, too. Because, *hello*, I was blindfolded and flirting with one of the robbers who'd taken me hostage.

But I instinctively trusted them. And I loved how wild and free they were. I wanted to have a name taken from a mythological god, and to be wild and free like them, if only for a little while.

Thor asked me more questions. It was so easy to talk with him, and soon I found myself describing the book of humorous essays I was writing, ironically entitled "Adventures in Sheep Farming," about life on a sheep farm. Someday I wanted to have real adventures and write about them. "Maybe 'Adventures in Sheep Farming' will be a best-seller and save the farm," I joked. "You never know."

"Your boss won't be foreclosing on your fucking-g farm today," Odin snarled from up front, somewhat threateningly. I liked how his threatening attitude was aimed at Hank.

"Why not?"

"That would look pretty fucking-g bad in the media, don't you think?" Odin said. "You get kidnapped from this guy's bank, and he decides to yank the family farm? You'll be able to milk this for at least a few weeks."

I sat up and leaned forward toward Odin. "You're right."

"Sit back." Thor yanked me back and scootched me down. "Stay low or I'll put you on the floor."

"Sorry," I mumbled, feeling happy and hopeful about the farm. I could milk this hostage thing!

In a matter of minutes, these three had accomplished what I'd been dreaming of doing for years: they'd royally messed with Hank Vernon and derailed the foreclosure.

"Or what if I stayed gone after you released me?" I said. "Get a job in nowheresville and make them sweat. As long as I'm gone, the farm would be safe."

"Yeah," Odin said sarcastically. "You'd be picked up in about two seconds."

"Well, I guess once you let me go, you don't really have a say," I said. "Maybe I'll try to stay hidden. I could send money home. He could never take the farm."

"Don't play games." Thor's voice sounded soft, but rumbly. "This business isn't as easy as it looks. Staying free, just walking down the street without having to look over your shoulder is worth more than money or a farm. We'll dump you somewhere, and you just play your hand straight."

It was here I got my new idea. "Okay, this might sound like a radical idea, but, how about if I tag along with you guys for a bit?"

A mean bark of laughter came from up front. Odin.

"No way," Thor said. "It's just...no way."

"I could be the wheel man. I'm a freaking amazing driver. Let me stay your hostage."

Thor chuckled softly.

I imagined the media. The Vernons would never be able to

touch the farm with me gone! Folks who disappeared from the Midwest got famous. People would probably send money. Maybe they'd start buying our Paris Hilton comforter. Maybe Paris Hilton would! Or Taylor Swift or Beyoncé!

I could find a way to secretly get word to my sisters that I was okay, somehow.

"You don't have a wheel man," I said. "What kind of gang doesn't have a wheel man?"

No reply. Had I hit a nerve?

My head swam with visions of adventures with a bank robbery gang. Maybe just a few months! We'd split the money we'd steal. It would be awesome. I'm not the kind of girl to steal money, but what if we only hit Vernon-owned banks? I would feel okay about that.

"You can't."

"Why not? I'm very brave."

Fingers softly grazed my forehead, brushing a lock of hair off my face. Thor. "There are *rules* to being in our gang."

Rules.

I don't know if it was the way he was touching me or the sexy rumble of his voice, but warmth flooded me at the idea of rules.

I was pretty sure they might be sexy rules.

I was not all that sexually adventurous in the real world, but this wasn't the real world. I was a hostage now. It was like a holiday from my life.

I swallowed, senses humming. "I have no problem with rules."

Thor said, "You might with these rules."

They say in sales that when a person starts voicing objections, it shows they're interested. Was Thor interested? Was he suggesting I might have problems with the rules because he hoped I wouldn't?

"Why would I have a problem?"

"We are a very well-oiled organization," he said, "demanding total obedience to the group."

Excitement surged through me. "You don't say."

"I do say," Thor said.

"That's enough," Zeus barked from the front.

"Right. Fine," Thor said. "Nothing personal," he whispered to me. This was the second time Thor had been reprimanded. Like he was the misbehaving ward of the two surly robbers.

"Is this about that scene in the safe room? I promise I was just performing for the microphone. I don't talk to myself like I'm two different personalities in real life. Pinky swear!"

"Put a sock in it." Odin sounded tense. "Trouble."

The van seemed to slow.

"Get down." Before I could move, Thor pushed me down on the seat. The top of my head smushed against the door, which was vibrating outrageously. Something warm was thrown over me. A scratchy blanket or something.

The guys were arguing. In my mind they looked angry and muscular and impossibly sexy.

Please let us get away, I thought. Yes, I was thinking "us" even at that point.

Somebody mentioned the bridge. Which one? I felt us turn and speed up. Had they hit traffic? Had there been a change of plans?

I stayed down, however. I wanted to show I was trustworthy.

More arguing up front. The van slowed. Thor swore. Odin barked to shut up. Zeus barked at both of them to shut up. It was then I knew what had happened.

I spoke up through the blanket. "You hit tractor pull traffic, didn't you?"

"Crap!" Thor said. "Tractor pull?"

"And you decided to take the bridge and it's worse," I added.

I felt the blanket get yanked off of me. The cool air was nice. I wished I could see.

"It was supposed to be yesterday," Zeus said accusingly.

"It got rescheduled for today," I informed the men. "Because of rain." Helicopter chops sounded above us. Sirens.

Odin said, "There was no notice of that. There is no fucking official policy of that. Nothing written."

Of course, when Odin said it, it came out as *no fucking gofficial policy of that.*

"It's just assumed," I said. "Everyone in town just knows."

"We're stuck with a hostage in a traffic jam?" Thor said.

"We should've dumped her at the train," Odin said.

"No, we should've known about this reschedule," Zeus retorted.

"Fucking-g small-town America," Odin said. "So we smash out. That is what God made hostages for."

"No, we sit tight," Zeus said. "They don't know this van."

"They'll figure it out," Odin said. "They'll come down the line and look in, and do you think a tied-up, blindfolded girl is gonna give us away? 'Cause I'm gonna go with a *Yes* on that." He mumbled something about bailing.

"Shut up and let me think," Zeus grumbled, power radiating through his words. The men shut up.

"I'm guessing we're on the Ganuck Bridge," I said. "FYI, boys, that river's shallow right now. In case you're really thinking about bailing. Don't do it. You'll crack your heads."

Mumbling from the front.

"We're on the bridge in a traffic jam, right?" I asked, wishing they'd just take off the blindfold. "With cops and a checkpoint up ahead?"

"Yup," Thor said softly.

"It could be a drunk check," I said.

"Nah," Thor said. "They're looking for us."

"And it's too late for me to leave the van now? I could stumble around and play dumb."

"Even if we trusted you for that, which we don't, there are too many witnesses to see you leave," Zeus grumbled.

"We're fish in a barrel," Thor said.

"Wait, they're looking for three guys with a girl hostage, right?" My pulse raced. "What if I weren't a hostage? Take my blindfold off. I'll sit in front like, *Hey, boys! We're late to the tractor pull!*"

Zeus snorted. But I heard nothing from Odin and Thor. "No go," Zeus said. "What's to stop you from giving us away?"

"The fact that I'm on your side? That I want you to get away with Hank's stuff? And also, you've been nice." Well, *Thor* had been nice. But it wasn't too late for Zeus and Odin to buy a clue.

Silence.

Were they thinking about it? My hopes soared like fun little birds.

Yes, these were bank robbers. But they were named after gods, and this idea fit my life's mission of saving the farm and my sisters. And taking more stuff from Hank Vernon would be a nifty side effect.

"Here's the deal," I said. "If the next bank we rob is a First City National owned by the Vernons and we split it four ways, I'll put everything I have on the line to get us out of this. I mean it." My voice sounded strange to my ears. "You're either shooting your way out of a traffic jam with a hostage, or you can let me help you."

"Even if you mean it..." Odin's voice. "You can't bluff us out. They'll have your picture. They're looking for you."

"I'm a woman. I can change my whole look. I can change my hair in two seconds if we have scissors. Anyway, they're looking for me the hostage. Ooh, also, they probably have my license photo, and it barely looks like me." Or at least, that's what I liked to think. "I'll talk us out of it—I know I can."

"Let's go for it," Thor said beside me.

"She thinks it's a game," Zeus growled.

Thor said, "You like our odds better in a hot exit with choppers above us? And she showed us the diamonds. So she tags along. It's better than a hot exit."

Hot exit. I was liking this outlaw lingo.

Odin said, "I'm going with Thor on this."

Zeus groaned, grudgingly.

"Two against one." Thor was already untying the blindfold.

"I'm in?" I whispered.

Hot breath in my ear. "Yup."

Chapter Three

I GRINNED AS HE PULLED AT THE KNOT. WE WERE GOING to do this! I was feeling better and better about this. I felt that the voting thing showed healthy mental balance.

"You'll be sorry if we start seeing police sketches of our faces after we let you go, Melinda," Zeus grumbled.

I was surprised they knew my name, but of course, it was right there on my badge. "I totally get it," I joked. "Police sketches are so unflattering!"

Thor snickered and whipped off the blindfold.

It took a while for my eyes to get used to the brightness. And the amazing hotness of Thor, with his creamy skin and wavy blond hair and velvety blue eyes. He wore a dove gray business suit, but even so, he looked more like a soccer player from Scandinavia dressed up for an interview. It was fitting he was named for a Norse god. I was guessing the big scowly guy with the short brown hair in the driver's seat was Zeus.

The handsome, unshaven, dark-haired guy in the passenger seat would be Odin. He wore squarish, scholarly-looking brown glasses, much to my surprise; I hadn't gotten "spectacles" from his badass mode of speech. And, let me say, the glasses looked awesome on him, and the small scar on his cheekbone was more like a tough-guy beauty mark than an imperfection. He was like a gorgeous model, which I guessed could be a problem in the robber line of work. Because who wouldn't stare at him? Who wouldn't remember him? His strategy for counteracting his runway model appearance seemed to be to swear a lot and seethe with bad-boy heat.

It just made him hotter.

Focus, I told myself, sucking in a breath.

I looked all around. Cars jammed the bridge in front and behind us; some of the people had gotten out of their vehicles. Frisbees flew through the air. Sirens and lights up ahead meant accident or police blockade.

"Cops are going car to car—I see a pair a dozen cars up," Zeus said. "We have maybe five minutes. They may interview you. Can you handle it?"

"So I'm in?"

"Perhaps we should alert her to the rules," Odin said.

Zeus shot Odin a hard look. There was something hunted and haunted about Zeus.

I was already taking off my stuffy gray bank teller jacket, wondering about these mysterious rules, and pleased I'd worn a skimpy, strappy white tank underneath, perfect for a tractor pull. I undid my bra and pulled it out from under my shirt.

"We're all going to the tractor pull," I informed them. "We want Big Bessie to kick ass. The three of you—suit coats off. Down to your T-shirts. And those slacks? Nobody wears slacks to a tractor pull."

"Unless they get suspicious, they'll probably only pull me out," Zeus said. "And you. They'll want to talk to you."

"Shit, this business skirt is so not right."

"I don't have a T-shirt," Odin said.

"No shirt is better than that one," I said. "Take it off."

The guys were stripping. Muscles were rippling. Sweaty skin gleamed. I tried to look all serious, but deep down I was like a lecherous little fish swimming in a delicious cocktail of testosterone and total freaking hunkiness. Yum!

Thor stuffed our suit jackets under the seat.

"They'll be looking for a girl with long red hair," Zeus said, handing back a hunting knife. "You wanna be in? You gotta lose the hair."

I took the knife. I knew he was right. "No scissors?"

"We're bank robbers, not beauticians."

Thor grabbed the knife. "I'll help you. This blade is sharp."

I pulled my long red hair out of my bun and shook my head. "I can't believe I'm doing this. I want you guys to remember how long and awesome my hair is, and how far out on a limb I'm going here. You better be good for your word." I took a deep breath, gathered my red hair into a ponytail at the back of my head, and showed Thor where to cut, then cringed. I could feel the hair weight disappear as the knife sliced through. He stuffed the hair into the pocket on the door. I said a silent goodbye.

"Avert your gazes," I said as I started wriggling out of my business-like black pencil skirt, down to my lacy underwear. When I looked up, Thor and Odin were watching me hungrily. Heat spread through me. Commanding the total attention of these devilishly hot bad boys was an off-the-charts turn-on.

"Maybe the god Zeus is the only one who knows what *avert* means."

Thor smiled wickedly. "We're bank robbers, baby. We make our own rules."

Ooh.

I put a flattened piece of box across my lap and laid my skirt over it, running the knife along the grain of the fabric, creating a quick mini skirt, trying not to smile. Zeus was right—I did feel like this was a game.

The best game ever.

"Thor, see if you can find any cooks' pants or anything," Zeus said.

Thor twisted around to root in the back. No use for other people's rules—it was so deliciously roguish. In spite of this—maybe it was their professionalism and sense of fairness, what with the voting—but I instinctively trusted them to follow their own rules, to be good for their word.

I held the skirt up. The hem was ragged in spots, but it would do as a mini skirt. I slid it back on. "Now I'm the only one who looks proper for a tractor pull."

Zeus turned in his seat to face me. He held a little metal box in his hands. "Show me your teeth."

I bared my teeth, and he opened the box and took out a small brown thing the size of a fingernail and held it up. Then he picked out a different one. "Hold still." He pressed it to one of my front side teeth.

"Smile."

I smiled. Odin laughed as I looked in the mirror. The little thing made it look like one of my teeth was dead.

"You have got to be kidding." But it was smart. My driver's license and bank ID photo showed a girl with all her white teeth.

Zeus shoved some mirrored sunglasses at me. "Put these on your head. The best thing is for you to hide in plain sight. Step out of the van, stretch your legs. Look down the line and see what kind of time we have."

I put the sunglasses on top of my head and pushed my now short hair behind my ears, then I climbed out into the bright sun. The door slid closed behind me. I stood outside the van, heat rising from the pavement, hitting my bare legs. We were in the very right lane behind a small gray car, and in front of that, more cars— four lanes of cars lined the bridge—two lanes heading north, two heading south, and none were moving.

I walked around the front of the van. In the lane to the left was another group going to the tractor pull—a bunch of teens in the back of a truck. They were drinking sodas and throwing fluorescent orange cheese curls at each other.

Some people looked my way, but I was pretty sure it was the outfit. It was sexy, what with the paper-thin spaghetti strap top that you could totally see my nipples through, and the ragged cave-woman mini skirt paired with my high heels.

It was like a different me stepped out of that van. Like a bad-girl butterfly emerging from a bandit cocoon.

I felt good.

I felt free.

I took a five-dollar bill from my still intact skirt pocket and walked over and offered it to the cheese curl kids in the back of the truck in exchange for two of their sodas. "Any flavor, I don't care," I said.

I came away with two Mountain Dews and some pitying looks from the girls for my dead tooth.

My blood raced when I caught sight of the cops, five cars ahead, talking to people and looking in cars. I rested my forearm on the open window and smiled in at Zeus, who was pulling on a pair of cutoffs.

"They coming?"

"Sure are," I said. The jeans shorts were just a little tight for Zeus. Un-Midwestern, but they were cops, not fashion police. "Four on foot, two with motorcycles."

"Move," he said.

I moved out of the way, and he got out of the van, shut the door.

Zeus had wide, muscular shoulders, a tree-trunk neck, and lush, handsome features.

I handed him a soda. He opened it and flopped an arm around me. "Don't fuck this up."

"Not planning to," I said, loving the feel of him, warm and hard against me. Loving his thuggish caveman vibe.

It was a vibe that probably made people underestimate his intelligence. I sure wouldn't. Not now, anyway.

He squinted when he drank his soda. "Hate this stuff," he said, looking casually around with those intense green eyes.

He was a handsome tough guy with the eyes of a feral animal.

His short brown hair twinkled merrily in the sunlight and curled wrong on the ends—it curled outward on one side and inward on the other, like the curl didn't get the memo that it was supposed to be symmetrical, and he'd never learned to properly manage it.

His whole primal thing was making me feel primal. Nobody had ever made me feel like that.

And of course I kept thinking about Thor's "skills" comment. And the rules. The well-oiled organization.

"Does my hair look not too fucked up?" I asked.

He gazed at me with those green eyes, and it was like a tremor through me. "It looks convincing enough."

I swallowed. "If you think you can sway me with flattery, you're wrong."

He looked away. I'd thought we had a connection, but he seemed wary of me now. He sipped his soda again, then wiped his mouth with his arm. Even that was badass.

"Look, you're doing great."

"Are you trying to build my confidence?" I asked.

"Yup."

"It ruins the effect if I know that's what you're trying to do."

He said nothing. Really, just having him close was heartening.

He had the calm power of a large animal, and his possessive arm over my shoulder felt weirdly reassuring.

I hadn't had a lot of boyfriends in my life, but those I'd had would've never thrown their arms around me in such a presumptuous and possessive way, and they certainly wouldn't have named themselves after gods.

He said, "Let me do the talking until you think I don't know the answer, then butt in. Let me see your tooth. Smile."

I smiled.

"Don't lick it."

I looked over my shoulder, into the van window. Thor and Odin were both lounging in the van doing phone things. Or at least pretending to.

One of the cops came to talk to the kids in the back of the truck next to us. Another pair of cops strolled up to us, both middle-aged men. One wore wire-rimmed glasses.

"There an accident up there?" Zeus asked.

I was amazed at how different his body language was, all hunched and frowny and bewildered. Like he was an oafish and victimy guy who would never in a million years rob a bank.

"Bottleneck," the cop with glasses said while his partner peered into the window. "Where're you off to?"

"Tractor pull," Zeus said.

"Who you rooting for?"

"Big Bessie," Zeus said. "If we even make it."

"You too?" the officer asked me.

"Bessie for the win." I raised my soda, heart pounding. "What happened? We're going to miss everything." I frowned. "Do you think they'll hold the main event?"

One of the officers shrugged, and I frowned harder.

Engines were gunning ahead.

"Drive safe," the one said. The two of them headed to the car behind us.

Zeus and I stood there together for a second. We'd done it!

Under my breath, I said, "Well, now I know what you think about the kind of people who attend tractor pulls. With that act you put on. You know, I go to tractor pulls. They're fun. They're not just for oafish bumpkins."

"Let's go," he said simply, straightening back up to his badass self. Maybe that's what they thought I was—a country bumpkin.

I walked around to the passenger side. Odin was there. "I think the girlfriend should sit up front."

Odin's darkly glittering smile set off quivers in the pit of my stomach. "The girlfriend sits where we tell her to sit. That happens to be one of our rules."

My pulse raced. The *rules*.

"The rules don't apply to Melinda," Zeus said.

The back door slid open, and I got in next to Thor and shut the door. I wanted to hear more about these rules, and I wanted them to be really dirty.

"Please," I said. "Call me Isis."

Thor looked surprised at this, and both he and Odin swung their gazes to Zeus, as if to see what he'd do. Zeus just stared grimly ahead. His silence brought a hush down over the van. The man's silence had power.

Finally I spoke up. "You all have god names. You said I could be in the gang until the next job. I think I deserve a god name. At least temporarily."

Thor seemed to pull himself together. "Thank you, Isis. You are awesome. That was awesome."

I pulled off my dead tooth thingy. Odin handed me the box and I dropped it in. There were other dead tooth thingies in there, plus tattoos, fake scars, and moles. "I can't believe you go around with a kit like this. Did you send away for it from the back of a comic book or something?"

Odin snapped the box lid shut. "Worked, didn't it?"

"We're not out of the woods yet, but—" Zeus caught my eyes in the mirror and nodded. "Thank you."

"Isis?" Odin said. "That's the name you're going with?"

"Isis is...I've always liked Isis. I know it's a terrorist organization, but how is it fair that they get to ruin an entire goddess's name, too?"

Odin snorted. "Not fair at all."

The cars in front of us began to move. Soon we were off the bridge and speeding along.

My pulse thundered in my ears, drowning out the hum of traffic and the distant *whop-whop* of police choppers.

They all had their shirts back on, but I was excruciatingly aware of their sexiness and their intense maleness, not to mention their dirty ideas. And every time one of them would talk, it was as if I could feel a rumbly echo all through me.

It was just the four of us. Alone. No more rules.

Zeus and Odin rumbled on about how the cops had handled the search like it was all very natural. Maybe it was a bandit thing.

I was far from natural. I put my hand over my chest. "Wow!"

"I know," Thor said, blue eyes sparkling. He seemed...aroused. It was exactly how I felt, like all my sex and danger circuits had crossed.

"What now?" I asked, holding his gaze.

From the front, Zeus said, "We lay down miles, change license plates and van decals, and then stop for the night."

Stop for the night. For some reason my mind went right to Zeus, to that moment in the bank when I touched his glove while handing off the bag, the frisson of shivers.

"And hit another First City? As a gang?"

"You're staying with us through the next job, we didn't say you could take *part* in the next job," Zeus said.

I sat back, disappointed. I didn't want to be the pesky little sister tagging along. I wanted there to be more.

There's this abandoned ski jump ten minutes from our farm, a creaky wooden thing built in the 1960s. It's so tall, you can see its dark bones cragging up into the horizon for miles around, beckoning you, *daring* you with its delirious height and rickety thrills.

When you drive over there and sneak up to it, you find a chain-link fence around it and *No Trespassing* signs all over, but it's easy enough to break in, easy enough to climb up it with your skis strapped to your back.

You just have to take care to avoid the rotten rungs.

Adrenaline and excitement build with every step, and then you're standing on top and there's nothing like it. You can see for miles around, and then you look down at the impossible downward angle, which tips up at the very end, designed to send you up into the air.

Standing up there before you push off is like the edge of ecstasy, like the still point at the tip-top of a roller coaster, and you know that you'll go.

Or more, you know that it will take you. That there will be a point of no return.

It's the most indescribable rush.

That's how I felt with the bank robbers—like I was standing on the edge of something wonderful. I didn't want to take off my skis and strap them to my back and climb back down.

"I have a question." I swallowed. "Why don't the mysterious rules apply to me? You said I was in. Shouldn't the rules apply to me as well as you guys?"

More silence.

Thor said, "Look, they're stupid rules we had once when our gang was different."

"It's important to me to play by the rules," I said, mouth going dry.

"You don't understand," Thor said.

Odin made a derisive sound and turned around in his seat so

that he faced back, staring right into my eyes. I couldn't begin to guess his background—Middle Eastern, Greek, North African. But let's just say he could slap on all the scars and moles and dead teeth from that box and still be hot.

"What?" I said, fighting the hypnotic effect of his gaze.

"Forget the rules," Zeus said from the driver's seat. "That's what. She's not playing."

Odin said, "She took a god name. She wants in. She already guessed what the rules are, or at least their nature." He paused, letting that sink in. It was unnerving that he was talking about me while looking at me.

Telling my secrets.

And also, I loved it.

I loved the out of control-ness of it. Like I was giving myself over to something powerful, something larger than me, the way I do on the ski jump.

My skin felt tight.

Odin said, "I'd say she has a pretty good *fucking-g* idea what the rules are."

My heart raced. "Is that so?"

"Very much so," Odin said. "And you wouldn't want it any other way."

I swallowed. What was this man doing to me? *I wouldn't want it any other way.* I crossed my legs, suddenly aware of the tickly energy there.

Odin raised his dark brows, as though my crossing my legs provided proof of his rightness. I loved the way he talked, the way he knew things, and I wanted him to say more.

Coyly, I said, "Well, I'd certainly like to know what the rules are so that I can evaluate them for myself."

I felt like I was starting a strange, sexy dance, and that somewhere deep inside, I knew the steps.

Zeus eyed me in the rearview mirror, all stern, bullish power. I felt Thor's eyes on me, too.

Heat radiated off of him.

My nipples drew tight—tight like they might punch right through my flimsy top.

I wanted to touch my nipples.

But even more, I wanted the bank robbers to touch them.

Chapter Four

"Well?" It seems customary," I began in my best bank teller voice, "that those who create rules would inform others of them instead of asking them to guess."

"Yes, that would be customary," Odin said darkly. "You really want to know? The rules of the game?"

"Yes, please," my straining nipples and I said.

"The game," Odin began, "is that we're depraved, sex-crazed bandits."

I bit my lip and nodded.

"The rules are quite simple," Odin continued. "Firstly, you must have sex with all of us at different times and in different combinations."

Gulp.

"That's firstly?"

It seemed like the kind of rule you work up to.

"Yes, Isis," Odin said. "Firstly."

I imagined being pressed between them. I imagined their hands and mouths on me.

"And what might be secondly?" I asked.

"That we get to tie you up. Etcetera."

Etcetera?

What was he not saying? What was the etcetera?

But I didn't want to seem like a rube, so I just nodded.

His brown eyes were like a caress on my skin. "And we give you various commands that you must obey. Within reason of course."

I could barely breathe.

"And we will call you Isis. You will only be Isis. But you can end the game and go back to Melinda at any time."

I nodded. I didn't want to be Melinda anymore. I wanted to be Isis and play their sexy game.

"You may be punished from time to time," he added.

"P-punished?"

"Sexy punishments that you would agree to, but they would be..." Thor's eyes sparkled. "Excruciating. But in a good way."

Erp.

"I'm sorry, but that's how it would have to be," Odin said, looking grimly at Thor.

Thor set a heavy, warm hand on my thigh. The pressure sent heat bolting through me.

I sucked in a breath.

"Do you understand why we might have to punish you sometimes?" Odin asked.

"I suppose." I was trying hard not to grin, but it was all so wonderful and hot. Somewhere back in Baylortown, Wisconsin, my sisters were probably worried out of their minds about me, but I didn't want to stop this roller coaster.

Maybe I couldn't stop it. But I definitely didn't want to.

"Fuck," Zeus said, shifting lanes.

I couldn't tell whether his commentary was about the road or about our conversation.

Gravely, Thor said, "We don't want to take away your name, Isis, but if we have to, we will. And you'll be Melinda again. If you leave the game." He scooted closer. "What do you think about the rules? Will you abide by them?"

I caught Zeus's eyes in the rearview mirror. What did he think about this?

"Did Thor just ask you a question?" Odin said.

My mouth was dry. Would I abide? I'd only ever had vanilla sex, and watched a bit of cartoon porn. They would laugh about the cartoon porn. I vowed never to tell them about the cartoon porn. I wanted Isis to be worldly.

"What's the etcetera? You said *tie you up, etcetera.*"

"The etcetera is decided as we go along," Odin said.

My pulse raced. I was starting down a ski slope into a wildly hunky unknown.

Thor cocked his head like he'd just realized something. "You're so into it."

"Yes," I breathed.

"Wow, Sherlock," Odin said. "Did you just now figure out how into it she is?"

"*We're* into it," Thor said. "Come here." He pulled me onto his warm lap, one hand on my hip, one on my thigh.

My sex ached. I wanted his hands all over me. Would we have sex now? It would be so outrageous.

"Say yes," Thor said, drawing one finger over my sensitive nipple, which was somehow more sensitive through the fabric.

"Yes." I was practically trembling out of my skin. "I'm in."

Something passed between Zeus and Odin—Zeus had given assent of some kind, with just his eyes.

Or did I just imagine it?

"I am going to have to ask you to do something for me," Thor whispered in my ear. "For us. It must be done."

We had exited the freeway now and were racing down a two-lane highway, heading south along the tracks. I melted backwards into Thor's lap, excited and, quite frankly, scared.

I dropped my hands to touch the sides of his thighs, enjoying the solidity of his muscles.

I thought about how he'd leapt over the teller counter.

What would he ask? I hoped it wasn't to suck all their cocks in succession. Even Isis wouldn't be into that, just on its own, at least without a sexy role-play context.

Odin was facing forward. Had he adjusted the mirror?

Thor ran his hands down my waist to my bare legs and then reversed direction, sliding upward, dragging his fingers heavily along my thighs, taking my skirt with it.

Slowly.

My skin heated under his fingers. Shivers skittered across my body.

His steely cock pressed against my ass. My core ached.

It had been so long since I'd had sex. I imagined discarding my panties, turning, pressing down on him, right there in the back seat, being watched. I had never done such a thing in my life. At least not while being watched.

Isis was so into it.

Up, up he went. Oh, God, he was going to touch me!

"Please," I breathed. "Please do." *And hurry*, I thought.

"You have to learn patience, Isis," he whispered, continuing up my thighs, hands heavy and rough in their excruciatingly slow march to rob me of my skirt. Eventually he had it bunched up around my waist like a belt with too much fabric. It was slightly demeaning, in a way that I liked. He hooked his thumbs under the elastic on my panties and snapped, "Off."

"Right here?" I said.

"Off."

I swallowed hard, liking how he'd ordered me. Probably best Melinda didn't think too hard about it. I shimmied my panties off, down to my ankles where they got caught on my high-heeled shoes.

"Assistance." Thor wrapped his arms around my chest and pulled me back to him.

Odin twisted around in his seat and reached back, taking one of my ankles, starting to dislodge my panties from my shoe while staring into my eyes.

Meanwhile. Thor played with my nipples, tugging them slightly outward.

Being touched by two men at once was beyond anything I'd ever imagined. And was Zeus watching? It was hard to tell, but even the possibility of it was a lust circuit overload.

My whole body trembled with excitement, every nerve ending madly exposed to them, straining for their touch.

Odin dislodged my panties—I couldn't see how because I couldn't seem to look away from his gaze, but there were yanks and possibly a rip involved. Odin didn't care about panties, and I didn't much care at this point, either.

Then he simply turned back to watch the road. Unless he could see me in the mirror...

"Go ahead," Thor said. "You know what you want to do."

"I want to do a lot of things," I whispered huskily.

"A hint, then." He grabbed my thighs and positioned my legs so that they were hanging over the outside of his legs; his movements were strong and sure, yet somehow tender. He spread his legs, which spread my legs even more.

I sucked in a breath as cool air kissed my bare sex.

My core clenched and throbbed. I felt so exposed to the front seat.

He kissed my ear and returned his hands to my breasts. "Show us how you do it."

I felt embarrassed to touch myself in front of these three guys, but I was also thrilled.

I took a breath and brought my hand down to my pussy—

tentatively—like it was somebody else's. Like I had to ask permission.

I slid a shy finger along my achy clit. The shock of contact made me gasp.

Thor exhaled deeply into my ear, a sharp tickle. "Yes." He'd enjoyed it, too.

He put his hands into my shirt and took hold of my breasts, rubbing his thumbs over my sensitized nipples, sending hot pleasure through me.

"Again."

Again, I stroked a finger through my silky folds. We both heaved hot breaths—there was a way in which it felt more intimate than having sex—me so exposed, so visible, my legs held apart by his legs.

And I was, of course, extremely wet. They would see that, too. I closed my eyes, concentrated on the feeling—Thor's hands on my breasts, my own on the folds of my sex, my every move revealed to my new bandit gang.

I bit back a moan and got into a little rhythm, stroking myself as Thor played with my nipples; sometimes he rolled them between his fingers like little beads, other times he tugged at them. Every new thing he did sent pleasure coursing through me.

I shut my eyes, blissing out, as a random scene from my cartoon porn travels came to me—an elfin cartoon girl tied up in the forest being ravished by roguish Robin Hood types, one fondling her breast, the other licking her sex, another watching. It was almost like that was really happening. And I would have an orgasm in front of them. While they watched!

But as soon as I thought that, some of the heat went out of me. What if I didn't come? Would they get bored of me? My orgasm was a very shy thing, easy to spook. And then suddenly I worried it *was spooked*. I opened my eyes, so self-conscious. "I might be getting stage fright," I whispered.

Odin turned with a dark gleam in his eyes. "Apparently I will have to do everything for this one." He took off his glasses and he bent his fingers backwards, one after another, as though to limber them up.

I widened my eyes. What was he going to do? Why take off his glasses and limber up his fingers?

His smile was evil. "Don't you stop now. You keep doing yourself. Or else."

"Or else what?"

"You'd disobey already?" he asked.

"No." I started again.

"No, what?"

"No...Odin."

"Good girl."

Good girl. I wanted him to order me around some more and say things like that. The way he looked at me, I knew he knew.

Then he turned his eyes down, and I swear I felt the weight of his gaze on my pussy. I slid my finger up and down, feeling so bare to him. The butterflies in my belly were going wild.

Thor's warm breath heated my ear. My tender nipples pebbled under his clever fingers as I touched myself.

And through it all, Zeus drove, silent as a mountain.

I rubbed my finger over my sensitive bud. My head felt light. My body was no longer mine; these guys were pulling me into a fabulous forbidden realm.

And I wouldn't have it any other way.

Again, Odin smiled his evil smile at me...or was he smiling at Thor?

Thor shifted me forward on his lap. I felt his hand on the small of my back. He pushed it down under my bunched skirt, down to squeeze and maul my ass cheek, then on down, nearing my vagina.

I panted, suddenly wanting—*needing*—him in me, his finger,

his cock. I wanted to fuck, to be fucked. Fear and yearning spiraled through my body.

Odin pulled off one of my high-heeled shoes and brought my foot up near his mouth, forcing me to raise my leg and bend my knee, giving Thor better access. Odin's breath was warm on my toes and a little bit ticklish.

Just then I felt a slick finger touch the entrance to my asshole. I gasped.

At that exact moment, Odin bit the fleshy tip of my little toe—just *bit into it.*

I cried out as I careened over the edge. "Oh my God," I said, losing myself in the sting of Odin's bite, and Thor's fingers, and my fingers, and an explosion of an orgasm. "Fuck!" I said, throbbing with waves of feeling from my eyelids to my toes.

"Ride it, baby," Thor breathed, slowing the motion on my nipple, caressing my ass cheek. I was so gone—my mind, my senses.

Shattered apart.

"Ride it." He slowed his hands, held me tight.

I rode it. Spinning.

I just panted when it was over, lolling on his lap like a rag doll. "Oh my God."

"And now we know," Odin said.

"Know what?" I breathed as Thor caressed my belly.

Odin put his glasses back on. "*Things,* Isis. We now know certain things."

"Like what?"

With one last devilish smile, Odin turned back to sit properly in his seat. "This will work." He shifted his gaze to Zeus, who continued to drive, all stern silence. Unsaid things seemed to pass between them.

What did he mean? Also, I was still thinking about the hand flexing.

You didn't need to flex your fingers to bite a girl's toe. Was it possible he had more things in mind?

Though it was possible Odin was the mindfucker of the group.

"That was hot," Thor whispered. "Thank you."

"Umm...you're welcome," I said. Though it seemed like I should be thanking them.

Now what?

I straightened my skirt, feeling totally weird about having just masturbated in front of them all. "What about you?"

"I want to take you so bad, I can't think straight," Thor panted.

"But we're in a van." Odin twisted around. "You didn't think we were going to just make you blow us all here in the van, did you?" He held out my panties and bra, looking amused. "And we'd hardly beat off in front of a total stranger. That would be uncouth, don't you think?"

I widened my eyes. Of course it was just what I'd done.

Or was he just joking?

"Shut up." I grabbed them from his hand and put my panties back on, and then my bra, back on under my shirt—no easy feat.

"Our needs are more complex than just jacking off," Odin said, adjusting his smarty-pants glasses.

Thor touched my hair. "We can wait," he said. "But we'll go slow. We don't want to freak you out or abuse your generosity."

"Yes, we do," Odin said. "That is exactly what we want to do. We want to abuse her generosity. And that's exactly what she wants. That is how the God Pack works."

The God Pack?

Thor threw an arm around my shoulders and glared at Odin. "Odin's fucking around."

"You will love the way we abuse your generosity," Odin said.

I caught Zeus's eyes in the mirror. Gaze grave, he said, "One week, and nobody does anything they don't want to, and then you go home while you still have plausible deniability. Got it?"

Nobody said anything more.

We sped through corn country.

It had been a wet, hot August and the crops stood high and thick, like short green walls, blurring by. Judging from the angle of the sun, it was dinnertime.

The mood of sex was still thick in the van, and I thought how frustrated these guys must be. My body still thrummed with energy; I couldn't let go of that moment when Thor was lewdly fondling me and Odin bit my toe. It was beyond hot!

Zeus said we'd stop for the night eventually. When?

And more importantly, what would happen? I had this feeling like the whole road trip was foreplay.

Chapter Five

"I SAW A SIGN FOR A FILLING STATION COMING UP," Zeus grumbled. "Area's looking okay to me. Anyone see anything?"

"Come here." Thor pulled me against him, pointing at the sky. "I'm looking for cameras. Look at the tops of the poles and anything on the wires. Describe what you see."

I nestled back into him. I could do that now. I was the girlfriend. We were the God Pack. It was weird they'd kept using their god names. Did they use them 24/7?

I described what I saw, shocked at how little I ever noticed about the poles and webs of wires and gadgets and barrel-looking things that had been right up there for twenty-five years. Thor told me the names and functions of the stuff, and what to watch out for, and I struggled not to wriggle in delight as his hands roamed possessively over me. Apparently there would be no sex in the van, though. Was that a rule? I needed a manual.

On my first day working as a bank teller, I was given a spiral-bound manual of rules and policies. I thought back on that, remembering the section on what to do in case of a robbery. I think you were supposed to put on the silent alarm and do what the robbers said, but I'm pretty sure they didn't have this mastur-bation scenario in mind.

"Always know where the eyes and ears are, wherever you go. Telephone poles are the worst. It's something you'll develop," he said.

Zeus grumbled. A warning of some kind.

That is how the God Pack works, Odin had said during his rules talk about how the woman must follow the rules.

So had some other woman come before me?

And if so, what had happened to her?

The three of them discussed the surroundings and various technological and geographical features they'd seen. Odin was reading things off some kind of alien-looking map on his phone. Was it a map of phone poles and cameras?

This whole finding-a-filling-station thing had turned the three of them from sex maniacs to five-star generals plotting a major invasion.

They started putting their businessman clothes back on, too.

Thor handed me my jacket. "It'll be good to have another pair of eyes. Being aware will be one of your jobs."

Again I got that sense of a ghost. A girl whose job it had been to observe things.

I recalled, just then, the stutter of attention on me when I'd taken a god name. Did the last girl have a god name?

"What are those green bell things?" I asked, pointing at a line strung between phone poles.

"Those are ceramic spacers. We'll have to do a whole tutorial on phone poles with you," Thor said. "That will be one of the only non-dirty tutorials you'll receive."

Shivers rained over my skin.

Apparently they were satisfied with this area. A few miles later, Zeus pulled into a run-down filling station whose concrete walls had vertical brown stripes near the top, showing the path of leakage from the metal roof. Junker cars crowded the edges of the lot and a lonely pump stood out in front.

A boy stood behind a counter inside, surrounded by cigarette displays. Zeus slapped down two twenties. "Forty for gas, and we'll take both flavors of bathroom keys."

Odin took both sets. "Let's go."

I followed him around the side of the station.

"You always get tons of high security with nice ones," he explained. "*Fucking-g* modern gas stations like *fucking-g* airports. We hate them."

I went into the bathroom with Odin's words ringing in my head. *Fucking-g airports. Gairports.* I really wanted to find out where he was from. I wanted to find out everything.

The bathroom wasn't so awful. I peed and cleaned up and finally got up the guts to look at my hair in the mirror. It was completely crooked, but when I shoved it behind my ears, it wasn't all that bad. But still, it needed work. I'd been thinking about getting it cut short, and maybe I could dye it pink. Isis would like pink hair.

When I came out, the van was on the other side of the station at the air pump. The side of it no longer said Romano's Catering; it said Marcomm Technologies in fat italic letters with two blue underlines. Odin loitered at the back of the van, partly concealing Thor, who was changing license plates. My bandits, like a bad-boy pit crew.

Soon we were back on the road, with Zeus driving again, and me in the back with Thor. I felt like I was in a dream, moving further and further away from reality, from my troubles. I liked it.

Odin threw us each a small bag of Doritos.

"Ranch," I said, my mouth watering. "Thanks." I was ravenous.

"We can't stop until Chicago, but we'll stay somewhere nice," Thor said with a little smile.

"Is that where you're from?"

"A few ground rules," Zeus said suddenly. "Don't ever ask us where we're from or how we got into this, and you can never know our names. Don't try to get that information, understand?"

"Okay."

"We took a leap of faith to trust you," he continued. "As you can imagine, it's not something we would have done normally, just pick up a stranger. But you were in a position to help us, and you came through, and that means something. We'll hold up our end of the agreement by taking down another of your boss's banks. Right afterward, we'll send you home with a plausible story that I don't want to have to work on right now. And we'll send your cut of the money to you somehow. And if you deviate from the story we develop for you, or if you don't do your re-entry how we say, we'll hunt you down and kill you."

The *kill you* seemed a bit harsh, but that was Zeus. Not a man to make empty threats.

Not a man to have empty sex, either, it seemed.

"How long until our heist?"

Odin snorted. "*Heist.*"

"It'll happen when it happens," Zeus snapped. "You have to be okay with not knowing the future. That is what this life is."

It sounded like the voice of experience. "And then you eject me?"

Zeus watched the road, not deigning to answer.

"It's better for everyone that way," Thor explained. "The longer you're with us, the less plausible it will be that you don't know anything and didn't see our faces."

"Right," I said, feeling suddenly upset at the prospect of being ejected—I'd only just become Isis! And, sure, I worried about my sisters, but I'd been dying on that farm. "It's just that, as long as I'm away, Hank won't take away the farm."

"Don't you care about people who might be worried about

you?" Zeus glared at me in the rearview mirror, which somehow seemed to amplify his disapproval of me.

"Of course I care," I said.

"Danger, subversion, and hedonistic pleasures," Zeus growled. "It's fun for a while, but at some point, you'll hit a low where you feel homesick. You don't want it to be too late to go back when that happens, got it?"

"Okay," I said.

"We're doing you a favor by dumping you," he added. "In the meantime, don't even think about getting a message to your people. You have to come to us with that sort of thing, and we'll decide what's smart. You need to tell me you get that right now."

"I get it."

"You think you've given the finger to every rule you've ever had to follow? You think you've seized a week of freedom and adventure? You haven't," he continued sternly. "You've traded in one set of rules for another. You've given up your freedom to the good of the group. We all have. That is how we stay strong. This is our power. It is a power beyond what you can imagine. Do not fuck with that power."

The guys all nodded, like they were all really serious about this.

"Okay." My voice sounded tiny to my ears. The silence that followed was almost thunderous.

This was more than a gang. More than bank robbers, I thought. They were three men living all together...this group must somehow form a family...I bit my lip. Bad time for the Brady Bunch song.

Also, what was up with the *danger, subversion, and hedonistic pleasures* bit? Who said that? Who *were* these guys?

Thor's cheekbones looked slightly pink, possibly from the sun, and he had blond scruff. He looked more like a tennis player than a soccer player, I decided. He said, "As far as you're concerned, we started our life of crime five hours ago when we hit your bank. We don't have a past or a future, okay?"

Odin looked back at me. "We're the fucking hive mind of crime," he said.

"Like the Borg?"

Thor gave me a heated look. "More like one for all and all for one."

My breath caught in my throat. "I never thought of that as dirty before."

He sat back. "This is a good time to start."

Chapter Six

I RESTED MY HEAD AGAINST THE BACK OF THE SEAT AS the scenery zoomed by, drowsily wondering what my sisters were doing. Probably entertaining police at the farm. Vanessa would bake cookies.

I'd talked a bit with Thor about it, and he said most hostages didn't get hurt. Hopefully the cops told them that. Or they could just Google it.

Maybe I could get a message to them. Zeus hadn't said I couldn't. *You have to come to us with that sort of thing,* he'd said.

More scenery zoomed by. I closed my eyes. The next thing I knew, I was face down on the seat with my cheek glued to the vinyl, with a hand gently shaking my shoulder.

We'd arrived.

I pulled myself together and we walked as a group across a parking lot and into the lavishly gold-gilded and palm-tree-filled entrance of the Regal Hotel.

I'd never set foot in a place so fancy. A lot of the money they'd stolen, I presumed, would be spent at the Regal Hotel.

Thor and Odin and I lingered in a stand of marble pillars and potted tropical plants in a corner of the lobby while Zeus went to the desk.

Thor and Odin had even put their ties back on. I supposed we looked like a group of businesspeople, aside from my ripped-hem mini skirt. They were the businesspeople, and I was the business-pauper.

"They don't need our IDs?"

Thor shrugged. "Nah. We're special."

"Gods?"

Odin settled into a posh velvet chair. "That's right, baby."

"So we lie low for a while?" I asked. "Is that the idea?"

Thor got a devilish look in his eyes. "That's one way of putting it."

My cheeks heated, and I didn't have to look under my jacket to know my nipples were hardening like two eager bullets.

"I love when you blush," Thor whispered. "I haven't even told you what we'll do up there, and you're already blushing. This is awesome already." He closed the distance between us and slid a finger down the side of my neck.

I shut my eyes. His fingers were like magic wands, but instead of fairy dust, he was sprinkling me with shivers of apprehension.

"Did you have something specific in mind?" I asked.

"Well, it's safe to say that first, you'll take off all your clothes," Thor said.

"Slowly," Odin grumbled from the chair, gaze cool on me. "Slowly, and one thing at a time."

"Is that so?" I said it a little bored, but really, I loved their dirty attention on me.

"Yes, Isis," Thor said. "It is so." He drew closer and kissed me, right there in the lobby, pressing me up against a marble pillar.

Every nerve in my body lit up, especially the extra-excited bundle of nerves between my legs where Thor's hard cock was currently pressing.

It was total exhilaration, this sudden, intense contact.

I wound my arms around his neck, enjoying the hardness of his body against mine, glad for the potted plants. Also, I enjoyed the idea that Odin was right there watching.

Thor pulled away. "You know you want to."

I took a deep breath. I wanted to feel more of this exhilaration. I wanted to feel more of his hard athletic body. As he kissed and nibbled at my neck, I made a mental note to ask him if he played soccer or tennis, but then the mental note ripped itself to shreds and drifted away and I just closed my eyes, wonderfully lost.

He whispered in his rough and silky voice, "Say you want to."

"I want to," I said. "What was the question again?"

He snickered softly. "Does it matter?"

"No." I gripped his necktie and looked into his eyes, face heating, pulse racing.

"But to recap," Thor said, "we'll tell you when you can take off all your clothes, and you'll do it. Slowly, or Odin will be extremely wrathful."

Odin glowered from his chair.

Wrathful!

"You'll bare yourself to us completely, Isis, and you must not try to cover yourself, even if you want to. When we're ready, you'll come to us. You will let us touch you everywhere we please. And don't think we weren't paying attention to your shameless display in the van. We'll spread your legs open wide just like that. Wider, maybe, and touch you like you touched yourself, but more. Far more. Because we have extra hands to use on you, don't we?"

He paused, seeming to want an answer. "Right," I said, wondering how many hands. I had the feeling it was just the three of us under discussion here, or would Zeus join in? I seriously wanted him to. Or would he watch, a silent mountain of a man with blazing eyes?

"Can you think of how extra hands could be an advantage?"

"Yes," I breathed.

"And what else do we have?"

Cocks, I thought. Did he really want me to say it?

"Oh, I know what you're thinking. You have such a degenerate imagination," Thor whispered. "What will we *impart?* What did we discuss in the van? I know that your mind was completely in the gutter, even then."

I smiled. "Skills."

"Skills you can't imagine. You would be shocked. And I have to warn you, we are relentless with our skills. Gods have no shame."

"*Thor* has no shame," Odin grumbled from his chair.

It was true. Thor had zero shame. I loved him right then. Him and his dirty talk.

Again, I wondered where these guys were from. Why were they robbing banks? They seemed highly educated and technologically savvy. They didn't at all have that hardened criminal vibe going.

"And this necktie you're clutching so hard?" Thor continued. "Can you think of what we might do with that? We each have one, you know. Ties are very strong material. Have you ever been in a position to find out exactly how strong a tie is?"

My mouth went dry. "No."

"Well, let's hope that you won't have to find out," Thor said.

Odin simply smiled his evil smile. Thor could get a certain mischievous grin, but Odin had an evil, glittering-eyed smile that made you feel like he was gazing right into your deepest, darkest secrets and lewdly violating each and every one of them.

I realized here that I was still gripping Thor's tie, knuckles white.

I let go.

Thor smoothed it against his chest without taking his blue eyes from mine. Even the way he smoothed the tie was suggestive. Then he brushed a chunk of hair from my forehead and placed a hand on the pillar next to my head.

His gaze made me feel naked, and I had the impulse to look away, like that would make me less exposed. Yet...I enjoyed it, too.

So I kept my eyes on Thor. I let myself be pinned by his gaze.

I let him know he had me.

He knew he did, and he knew I knew. It was a total rush.

"A tie has several uses for a squirmy goddess, you know," he continued huskily.

My breath sped. I locked gazes with Odin, who was sprawled on the lobby chair like a surly prince.

Thor continued, "A tie is very useful on a squirmy goddess whose body we are using for our *complete and utter satisfaction*."

Naturally he managed to infuse the phrase *complete and utter satisfaction* with tons of dirty significance. I stood there, pinned like a helpless butterfly to a cool marble pillar. Pinned by his deep blue eyes and his dirty talk.

"Do not forget about the hot tub," Odin said. "Hot tubbing has its many aspects."

"Oh, yes," Thor continued. "Many aspects. Have you spent much time in hot tubs?"

I shook my head.

"Well, you will now. You'll get to know all about hot tubs. But we'll see what the layout is like. Things sometimes have to flow organically from the layout. We let the layout speak to us. I'm sorry, but there's not always a lot we can do about it."

Flow organically from the layout? Let the layout speak? I stifled a grin. "Are we going to have sex or do feng shui up there?"

"Oh, dear," Odin said. "Sounds like Isis is getting a bit out of line already."

My blood raced. I swallowed and glanced toward the front desk just in time to catch Zeus striding across the lobby, all brutish grace, briefcase in hand.

To the people in the lobby, he probably just looked like a well-off traveler and not a really powerful bank robber, but I could see him now.

I could feel him.

He held my gaze.

The press of his silent dominance got heavier as he neared, but there was something else as well—a cold light in his eyes that felt like accusation.

Did he really not want me there? Or was I imagining it?

He looked away only when he reached us. "Come on, party people."

I followed the three of them to the elevators, knees weak.

Zeus punched the button for the top floor, and we rode the elevator to our room like normal business travelers and not three bandits and their hostage about to have a wild ménage.

Or maybe this was how bandits about to have a wild ménage rode an elevator, all stern and silent before the event.

How would I know? I was raised on a sheep farm.

Odin caught my eye and smiled knowingly. I looked away from him, just stared ahead at the button panel with probably a dorky expression. I felt like I was trapped in a state of suspended erotic animation. None of us were fucking or even touching, but I was so aware of these men, wound so tight with horniness, even the elevator bell tweaked my nerves.

Then the doors slid open.

Thor set a hand on the small of my back and guided me out the elevator and down the hall to our room.

Zeus shoved the key card in and out of the slot and yanked the door open.

Chapter Seven

My pulse raced as we walked into our hotel room —Zeus, Odin, and me, followed by Thor.

Or make that, walked into our hotel *rooms*. We had a mammoth suite with two wings of rooms—bedrooms, presumably—and in the center, a posh and rambling living area with velvet and marble furnishings, velvet curtains, and a massive hot tub.

Zeus went immediately into one of the side rooms and slammed the door.

"Is he okay?" I asked.

"You have to leave him to himself. He needs to exercise and be in his cave a while." Thor dropped his bags and came to me. "Zeus has his own timetable." He slid his hands over my shoulders.

"Okay," I said.

A knock at the door. Thor broke away from our kiss. A room service waiter pushed in a cart laden with booze, glasses, snacks, flowers, and linens. "Would you like me to set you up?"

"No, just park the cart. Leave the table clear. Just in case."

The waiter parked the cart next to a marble table.

Odin took off his glasses and gave me an amused look that had 99% pure devil in it. "Don't you think?" he asked me.

"What?"

"That we should leave the table clear?"

"I guess," I said.

WTF.

Odin gave the waiter a couple of fifties. As soon as the door closed, Odin unscrewed the cap from the bottle and poured three shots. He handed one to me and one to Thor. He downed his and loosened his tie, eyeing me lewdly.

My nerves skittered.

Would we just start now?

Usually I changed clothes after I traveled. I supposed I would now. Or at least take them off.

I gulped down my scotch. It burned warm in my throat, roasting my chest from the inside.

"Frightened?" Odin asked.

"A bank heist followed by group sex isn't my normal schedule, that's all," I said breezily.

"Oh, one of the best things about you is your pretend confidence," Odin said.

"It's not *pretend.*"

"Thor likes your embarrassment, but I like your pretend confidence." Odin gestured for me to hold out my glass and he poured me another shot. "We'll enjoy stripping them both away."

I laughed nervously, heart pounding out of my chest. "Umm..."

Odin didn't laugh.

Thor didn't either. He just watched me with that butterfly-pinning gaze of his.

I had nothing to say, so I drank my shot.

My heartbeat fluttered in my throat as he strolled over and took my glass from my hand. "That's enough of the talk. Come on." He led me over to the main seating arrangement, velvet couches and a couple of giant chairs, then threw himself into a couch. "Strip."

Odin sauntered over with his glass and leaned his elbows on the back of the couch, looming behind Thor.

I felt so nervous, just standing there in front of the two of them. "Just like that?"

"It's typically how this thing starts," Odin said.

I unbuttoned my jacket, face hot. Would Zeus come out soon? Would he be angry we'd started without him, or did he not care?

"I love this already," Thor said. "I love how nervous you are."

"I'm not nervous."

Odin got a stern expression. "Lie about how you feel again and it'll be trouble. A punishment, Isis. We let the feng shui bit go, but don't think we're easy."

I sucked in a breath. His stern tone made my pussy quiver. His gaze felt like metal on my skin. I could barely work my fingers on my jacket buttons.

Odin didn't smile. He just watched me with that smoldering, ultra-male attitude. I took off my jacket and tossed it.

His expression didn't change even a little bit.

I watched Thor for the next part. I touched my breasts the way I imagined a stripper would, wanting to show I wasn't some nervous girl from a sheep farm, even though that's what I was. I pulled my shirt off and tossed it behind me.

"Your skirt next," Thor whispered.

I pulled my skirt down and stepped out of it, so that I was wearing only a bra and panties and my high-heeled shoes.

I felt everything on my bare skin—the men's gazes, cool air currents from vents unseen. Even the light from a neon sign somewhere out there in the dark night beyond the window had a sensation to it.

I ached to be touched.

"Pull your bra down under your tits," Thor said.

I sucked in a breath and pulled down the lace. It made my breasts stick out way more than they normally would. Like my breasts were offered up on two little trays for the pleasure of these dangerous strangers.

My pulse sped. My cheeks burned, and the flush spread all the way down to my breasts.

"Oh, this is good," Thor said. "Now come here."

I went to him on trembling legs. Thor put down his drink and pulled me to his lap, making me straddle him, one knee on either side of him.

Gently, he brushed a hand over my breast, over my nipple. Electricity cascaded through me, right down to my pussy. "You're blushing and it makes me want to devour you like a cupcake."

He leaned in and sucked my nipple with harsh, jolting force. Just when it was almost too much, he stopped and blew cool air on it. He started twirling the other gently between his fingers.

"Oh my God," I panted.

Five seconds in, and my mind was melting. And they knew it —I was sure of it. These were two very sexually devious bandits.

Suddenly, Thor rubbed the flat of his tongue over my diamond-hard nipple.

"I think I might come," I hissed, grabbing his hair.

"Not yet." Odin came around and pushed his hand down the back of my panties. He squeezed my ass cheek. Then he brought his other hand around to cup my sex, sending ripples of pleasure through my pelvis. "No coming. Not until we say so."

Oh, so it was going to be one of *those* deals.

Odin squeezed and massaged, making me writhe. His touch was brutal and tender, both at the same time.

Thor caressed my stomach, nibbling and sucking my breast.

Odin kissed my neck as he pushed his hand down the front of my panties—inside now—touching the slickness between my legs. He grabbed my hand and put it over the bulge in his pants. I reached down to touch Thor, too. He growled into my nipple as I squeezed his shaft through the fabric of his gray slacks.

I know there were only four hands on me, but it felt like a dozen, touching and exploring me, pinching and teasing, sending me into bliss overdrive.

Pleasure thrummed through me in waves.

If anything, Thor had undersold their skills. I never knew where their fingers would roam next, and eventually I gave up tracking any of it. I moved in a rhythm against somebody's hand. I rubbed two cocks through two pairs of pants. It was like I was in a sex kaleidoscope.

The pants needed to come off.

Would they want to have anal sex? I never had, but Isis would go for it. I wanted to give these men everything they demanded. New pleasure swelled in my belly at the thought of them bossing me around and demanding things.

"Christ, I could come right now," Thor said. "I want to take you so hard, but I just don't know if I can decide how. I want to fuck you all night."

Please do, I thought.

"Come here." Odin pulled me backward and I stepped back off the couch, off Thor. "Take off his pants and suck him," Odin whispered in my ear.

I kneeled in front of Thor and started to undo his belt.

"No, not like that." With his hands on my hips, Odin pulled me up to stand again, and then kissed my ear, warm and breathy, and he whispered softly, so that only I could hear, "Don't kneel; bend. I want you bent over and totally open to me. I need full access to your incredibly wet pussy for what I have in mind right now."

Heat built between my legs. I started to form a funny reply, like how full of helpful suggestions he was, but then he shoved my panties down off my hips and the quip melted away.

"You've never been with two men before, have you?" Odin asked. "Tell the truth."

"No," I admitted, figuring that he already knew.

"That's perfectly fine," he said.

Thor groaned. "Better than fine. We're gonna break you in so hard."

"Now bend over," Odin whispered into my ear.

It was harder to bend down to Thor than to kneel in front of him, but I planted my hands on the couch cushions on either side of him and supported myself that way. Odin held my hips, fingers pressing into my flesh.

"Good girl," Odin said. "Now spread for me." He nudged the inside of my ankle with his foot, forcing me to spread my legs apart. I planted my feet wide, still balancing on those high heels.

"Excellent, Ice."

A lone finger touched my sex and a bloom of heat spread out through my belly and my butt.

The devious finger slid along my sensitive bud, down along my folds, and then slowly back. I hissed out my pleasure, sure I was going to orgasm.

"Thor, take off your pants," Odin commanded, sliding his finger along my seam again. I gripped the couch. The floor felt like it was dipping underneath me.

Thor pulled off his pants.

"Oh," I said as his giant cock sprung free, golden like the rest of him, with a shining dot of liquid on the tip. I wrapped my fingers around the base of his dick and, one hand planted firmly next to his hip, I slowly, lustily, licked off the drop.

"Yes," Thor breathed. "Yeah. Put your lips over me. Take me, Isis. Take everything."

Odin continued to finger my seam as I lowered my lips over

Thor, swirling my tongue around him. Thor teased my nipples with his fingers, and my heart stuttered as I felt a finger sneak into my cunt, then out, then two in.

I took Thor halfway into my mouth as Odin touched and explored me. Heat ran thick through my veins.

"You can't stop," Odin said. "You can't stop until we tell you."

And I would ever want to, why? I thought, but my tongue was busy on the underside of Thor's cock, so I just made an *mm-mm* sound.

In my experience with cartoon porn, I found it not that erotic when elfin girls had to blow guys while getting fucked, but I could see now that I'd been horribly wrong in my thinking, and I really wanted to try that now.

But that thought broke apart as the three of us got into this amazing rhythm, and I didn't really care if we were fucking or fingering or what.

A door somewhere opened.

Zeus!

I stilled.

"Keep going," Odin whispered. "Don't stop."

But Zeus was right there at the side of the couch, speaking with Odin casually about going down to the workout room. I'd been excited for Zeus to come out and join in, or at least watch, but not this, acting like I was a lapdog or a piece of furniture.

I pulled my mouth off Thor, feeling embarrassed and flustered, and straightened my arm, so that, okay, I was still bent over, but not sucking on Thor's cock.

Zeus wore sweats and a tank top and a towel flung over his shoulder, clearly on his way to the hotel gym. He said something about dinner, even as Odin continued to drag a finger slowly up and down my wildly alert seam.

"Call me on the zero," Zeus finally said. He glanced at me coldly and then left.

The silence in the room was broken only by the click of the door being shut.

"Awk-ward," I said.

My two swains said nothing.

"What?" I said.

Thor knit his brows together, as though something troubled him. "Did you disobey a direct order just now, Isis?"

"W-what?"

"Did you follow all of Odin's directions just now? Or did you disobey?"

Odin had stopped his exquisite fondling. He rested his hands lazily on my hips, and I could feel his cock tipping at my ass crack.

"Well, but—" I wrapped my fingers around the base of Thor's cock.

Thor shook his head sadly and dislodged my fingers. "Do you remember Odin's command to keep going? But instead, you stopped while we had our discussion with Zeus? Do you think that was a good example of obedience?"

My pulse raced. "I remember exactly where we left off."

Odin took hold of my arms and pulled me up. "Up."

"What?" I stood. I couldn't believe they wanted to cease and desist. "Come on."

Thor said, "You agreed to obey, yet you didn't. We need to be a perfectly disciplined group of criminals, or we have nothing. Do you understand that? We have nothing without discipline. This is something you need to learn if you're going to stay with us."

"But—" I laughed at the bonkers-ness of it all. "To be practically fucking while you have a discussion?"

"You said that you would obey, and you didn't," Odin said. "Now thanks to you, all of our lighthearted fun is over."

Lighthearted fun? That was lighthearted fun?

Thor stood. Odin kept hold of my arms.

I felt the breezes of the room on my belly and on my madly

pebbling nipples, straining at the ends of my breasts, which pointed forward in a shamelessly bullet-like way, thanks to the pulled-down bra supporting them underneath.

I felt almost giddy with excitement. "But after our day, don't we deserve some lighthearted fun?" I was getting into being Isis. Isis was a little bit disrespectful. Isis needed some structure.

"We do deserve fun." Odin came around the front of me and yanked his tie off his neck. "Don't worry, we'll enjoy this, too. Well, Thor and I will." He tied the end of his tie to my right wrist.

Eep.

Was I going to allow this?

Yes, I *so* was.

Chapter Eight

"WHAT ARE YOU GOING TO DO?"

Odin held my gaze with his brown eyes and touched the tip of his finger to the bottom of my chin. "Nothing you can't put a stop to. Just say...Mississippi."

"Mississippi?"

"Do you have a problem with that?"

"No."

Odin said, "Untie Thor's tie for him, then."

I reached up and untied the knot in Thor's tie and slowly pulled it free of his collar, heart racing like mad.

"Thank you," Odin said as Thor tied it to my left wrist.

Then Odin yanked off his belt.

Gulp. "What are you going to do with that?"

"You'll see."

"You're not hitting me with that."

"Is that a Mississippi?" Odin asked. Thor, too, had his belt off.

I thought about this. They'd said the rules were for our mutual pleasure. So far, they had been. In fact, I felt I was getting the most pleasure.

Odin tied my wrists together—pretty tightly. I could probably get out. *Maybe.* Still, I didn't like the belt aspect. "I'm not sure about this."

"Are we doing anything right now that you object to?" Odin asked.

"Well—"

"At this *very* moment?"

"I guess not at this very moment."

"Come here, then." Odin led me to the table by the tie. I felt a little bit like a horse, but in a hot way.

"Bend over the table," Odin said from behind me. "On your elbows."

I could barely breathe as I bent over it, holding the edge of the table with my tied hands, breath ragged.

If I don't like it, I will say Mississippi, I said to myself. I waited, ass exposed, nipples nudging against the cool marble with every breath I took.

Thor grabbed hold of my hair and turned my head to the side he stood on, kneeling so that we were face to face. "It always goes better for the fucking when you don't disobey." He ran a finger over my cheek, and then he stood and went around to the front of me. He took the ends of the ties binding my wrists and tied them somewhere underneath. Maybe to the table legs?

Odin ran his hands over my totally displayed ass. "That's right, we get to the fucking so much sooner when you're disciplined."

"I guess *so*," I whispered.

Behind me, Odin continued to caress my ass, now with two hands. "Are you being funny? Was that a smart remark?"

I turned my face down to the table, forehead pressed to smooth marble, adrenaline coursing through my veins. "Sort of," I admitted. This was more intense than all the extreme sports I'd ever engaged in—all put together!

Thor kneeled in front of me. "Hey."

I looked up at him.

He was shaking his head sadly. "That merits a double punishment." He looked above my head, up at Odin.

"What?"

"We need obedience, Isis," Odin said. "You understand why we have to do this? When you delay our pleasure like this? One person can't be allowed to mess things up and then mock our process." He paused. "Say, 'I understand and accept my punishment.'"

The butterflies in my stomach were going wild. I was really supposed to say *that*?

"Say it." Odin scratched a fingernail along my butt cheek, leaving a wicked line of heat that sizzled into me.

I gasped.

It was here that I understood something about being tied up— every little touch contains a world of feeling because you can't stop it. My body hummed. My senses stood at attention. What would he do next?

"Say it."

"I understand and accept my punishment," I whispered. *And there is always Mississippi*, I thought.

A hush. Thor stood.

That's when I felt the cool leather against my ankle. It was Odin, winding the belt around my ankle. Phew! So that was the plan! I felt the belt tighten, binding my leg to a table leg. I was relieved when he used the other belt to tie my other leg to that same table leg, which left my legs somewhat strapped up together.

I had hoped to have the fucking part of the night start, but apparently that wasn't on the agenda at this point. But at least the belt whipping part wasn't going to happen either, what with both belts occupado.

Still, my imagination raced. Would they actually spank me? What would it feel like? I gripped the table edge so hard my knuckles went white.

"Close your eyes and put your forehead back down on the

table," Thor said. He was standing right in front of me. "We don't want you getting distracted from your punishment. You need to feel this in order to remember."

As if I wouldn't remember. But I complied.

Out of nowhere, I felt the sharp sting of Odin's hand slapping my ass. I gasped.

It stung. Though I didn't know how much of the sting was just the shock.

And then he did it again.

Hard.

Okay, it stung-stung.

And then again.

My ass vibrated.

Hot, wicked pleasure speared into the achy place between my legs. I didn't know what to think about it. My mind didn't have a box for this strange pleasure-pain.

He did it again, harder.

"Uh!" I cried.

"Was that Mississippi?"

"No," I whispered.

"So you want more?"

I swallowed.

"Say it," Odin commanded. "Spank me again until my punishment is complete."

I resisted making the joke I could've so easily made there. "Again."

The silence stretched out. I waited.

Waited.

Why was nothing happening?

"Full sentence," Odin said.

"Please," I whispered, ready to weep from the mental strain of them not doing things to me. I felt bereft, tied up there. I needed to be more...something. Anything. "Please spank me until my punishment is complete. Until you are *utterly and completely* satisfied. *Utterly.*"

With that, his hand came down on my ass. I sucked in a shuddery breath, forehead pressing into the smooth tabletop, hands gripping the edge.

I lived for that exquisite feeling on the end of each spank, that sweet reverberation sailing into my clit.

I ground my pelvis into the edge of the table as he spanked me. My sex clenched and released. I could orgasm just from this.

Odin stopped and slid a rough hand over my tender ass cheeks. Even that—Oh! I felt everything.

Was it over? I panted. I could feel a drip of cool sweat rolling down from my underarm, down onto my breast, tickling it.

"Mmm," Thor whispered. I'd forgotten he was in front of me. I felt his finger trace the path that the drop of sweat had traced down my breast, right to where it squished against the table. He found my nipples, squeezing and plucking at them.

And then Odin slapped my ass again. And he kept on, hard, then soft. And a pluck, a tweak, a caress on my breasts. My ass. We got into this rhythm, and my mind got all messed up—I felt like we three were fucking, just in this. I had lost all sense of everything.

And then I felt Thor's hands in my hair. He turned my head. He'd stopped with the breasts. I opened my eyes, feeling drugged.

He looked as wild as I felt, skin flushed, pupils dilated. Cock hard. "Good. Take her right here or I will."

"Please," I said. "Take me. Or I will!"

Thor snorted and untied my wrists with frantic energy, and then untied them from each other, though the ties were still on them. Like wrist leashes.

Odin unbuckled my legs. "You don't think this is the best part?"

I turned over and he rose up and pulled me up against him

into a kiss. He wore only his white businessman's shirt, hanging open, and a condom.

I thought I would die as his cock probed and moved along the seam of my pussy.

I shoved my hand into his dark, moppy hair as we made out. "I want you in me so bad."

Either one, really, but it was Odin's cock at the gate. My heart beat at probably an unhealthily high rate.

Odin pulled away. "Don't you have something to finish first?" He turned his head. I followed his gaze. There was Thor, back on the couch.

"Oh, right." I was, of course, happy to get back to that. In fact, it almost blew my mind that I'd be allowed to.

Odin grabbed the leashes of my wrists into one hand and led me over. It was as erotic the second time as it was the first.

"And you don't stop this time. Even for an earthquake. Got it?"

"Got it."

I had this impish thought to start and stop anyway and see if they would go through the spanking thing again.

Except not.

"Bend over. Nicely."

I bent over Thor on the couch yet again, trying not to smile as I wrapped my fingers around his perfectly hard, huge cock.

"Yes," he said, putting his hand on the back of my head.

Naturally I'd made sure to keep my legs somewhat together as I bent over because I wanted Odin to make me spread them again with that kick.

Odin did not disappoint. Roughly, he kicked the inside of my ankle, sending shivers skittering over my skin. "Spread. Wide," he commanded roughly. "Now."

I complied.

Slowly, I took Thor into my mouth as Odin touched my ass all over and even slapped it once, which made me gasp and nearly choke on Thor's cock. I supported my weight with one hand and grabbed Thor at the root with the other, rubbing up and down as I sucked.

Odin's hand snaked in front of me now, fingering my tender, throbbing bud. My breathing went rough. I didn't know how I'd keep from coming if he entered me.

"Make her come while she's got me in her teeth and you're a dead man," Thor said. "No offense, Ice, but you might be a biter."

I grunted, a kind of *nunh-unh*.

"Shhh," Thor said. "More."

I could see that he was on the edge, so I concentrated fiercely on him, sucking and rubbing, trying desperately to ignore Odin's confident fingers sliding around on my sex.

I could understand Thor's nervousness, since we'd only just met today.

The base of Thor's dick thickened even more, and he clamped his hand onto the back of my head, forcing me to still, and he let out a cry as he pumped his cum into my throat, which I swallowed.

Naturally, Isis was into it.

Everything seemed to slow.

Even Odin slowed, maybe in honor of Thor's orgasm.

Thor slowed and stopped, panting.

Thor's hand rested limp in my hair. I gently pulled away from him.

"Oh, Isis," Thor said, stroking my hair. Then he grabbed it in a bunch and brought my head to his and kissed me. "Oh, that was good," he whispered.

I rested my arms around the couch back, around his neck, and kissed him as Odin pressed his cock at my seam, sliding it back and forth across my wetness. It felt so good. And then he guided himself into place, and with one hand planted firmly on my hip, he entered me.

Slowly.

Excruciatingly slowly.

I dropped my head to Thor's shoulder. I couldn't multitask anymore, I just needed this. Thor tweaked my nipples as Odin invaded me, right to the hilt.

I gasped. He was huge, almost too huge. I was full up to my eyeballs.

Gradually, Odin pulled out, then he pushed in again.

"Do it," I gasped. "Do everything."

"Good girl," Odin said, reaching around to the front of my pussy to rub my clit as he thrust into me.

I hissed out a breath. Now I had all these hands on me *while* being fucked. Deliriously, I backed up to him, needing more and more and more. Totally on the edge.

"Yeah," Thor whispered. "Take him. Give it all up."

Odin's fingers sped wickedly, and then Thor took hold of my nipples and twisted them, sending shock waves through my core. "Give it up, come for us," he whispered.

It was mercy that he said that—I was coming already, wave upon wave of the most pleasurable, blinding orgasm I'd ever experienced. I cried out, my senses hurtling through dark space. Odin held my hips more firmly, his cock pushing into me, relentlessly, breaking me apart, and I realized he, too, was coming. He clenched my hips and thrust one last time, locking deep inside me, cock pulsing.

I cried out, unable to process, as my orgasm swelled through me.

"Yes." Thor caressed my hair, kissing the top of my head, practically making out with it.

Some moments passed. I barely knew where I was.

"Jesus," Odin whispered, as we sort of came down together. "Jesus." He pulled out.

I turned and collapsed next to Thor. Odin went over to discard his condom in a wastebasket and then collapsed on the other side of me.

"Wow," I said.

Odin kissed my ear. He grabbed both my hands and kissed my fingers. I smiled and then I lay sideways over Thor's lap, still holding Odin's hands.

"I can't believe how amazing that was," I said.

The three of us sat like that for a while, basking.

Thor reached over, picked up the phone, and called room service.

To order food.

Guys.

I realized I was hungry, too. "Oh my God, I'm starving!" I announced. I'd eaten nothing for hours.

Thor handed over two menus.

I flipped my legs up across Odin's lap so that I was lying across them, and I read my menu from that position. The prices were exorbitant.

Odin put in his order; he wanted two steaks. Thor added on two lobsters and a large pepperoni pizza, chocolate-covered cherries, an entire flourless chocolate cake, and two bottles of champagne.

I paused over the menu's description of the mushroom burger, my sister Candy's favorite food in the world, feeling a flash of guilt for how much fun I was having. All my life on the sheep farm I'd had this sense that all the excitement was happening elsewhere. Now I'd found that place. Even so, I told myself I'd be home soon.

"Hurry up," Thor said.

I decided on fettuccine Alfredo and a mini pizza. "I can't believe none of us have eaten since those gas station chips." I handed my menu back to Thor.

"It's the job energy. Doing a job produces all this *fucking-g* energy. You can't eat, you just want to fuck, but after you fuck, then you must devour everything."

Thor stroked my hair. "Though we like to repeat the fucking and eating cycle a lot between robberies."

"What would you have done if I wasn't here?" I asked.

Odin gave me a warning look that sent shivers through me. "You know what they say about curiosity and the cat."

This only made me twice as curious. Did they pick up women? Hire prostitutes? Have sex with each other?

"We're glad you're here," Thor said.

"I am, too," I said. "I am totally into your bandit cycle."

Thor looked down at me. "I am totally into you."

I smiled up at him. "I am totally into you." I gazed over at Odin. "And you." It was weird being three.

Odin twisted his lips in a mocking smile, ejected my legs from his lap and stood, but not before I caught the warmth in his brown eyes. He strolled over to the hot tub, shedding his white business-man's shirt, and stood at the edge, fully naked, his smooth brown skin lighter over his perfectly toned ass.

I wondered again about Zeus. How did he fit in?

They hadn't seemed to expect him to join. Is this how it would be for the week? Zeus all distant?

I'd felt such a fierce connection with him at the bank, but now that I was in, he could barely tolerate me.

Chapter Nine

"Come on," Thor said, getting up from the couch and heading for the hot tub.

I wandered over to the liquor cart and grabbed a handful of pretzels as the two guys sank into the tub. It was here I noticed the flowers had been reduced to just stems, with a few ragged petals hanging off.

"What the hell happened to the flowers?" I asked.

"Zeus," Thor said darkly.

"Oh," I said. His tone told me that a follow-up question might not be the thing.

We took a dip in the hot tub while we waited for our food.

The thing was massive—the size of two king beds—and surrounded by marble. I rested my head on the side of the pool, letting the jets hit my back and allowing my body to float, letting all the tension drain away. I learned this was one of my bandit boys' favorite hotels.

I got the feeling they were fancy hotel connoisseurs.

"Isn't it expensive?" I asked. "To stay in this suite? I mean, sure, bank robbers make a lot of money, but wouldn't it be prudent to save some for the future?"

"The bank robber lifestyle is high stakes, high reward," Thor said. "You can't go skimping on the reward part of the equation."

"It's the opposite of a farm," Odin added. "We're into maximizing today, not tomorrow."

It was so poignant. Sad, even. Like they didn't see a future for themselves. How had they come to this?

Did they plan to go out in a blaze? I hoped not.

Well, it was definitely the opposite of a farm. On a farm, you were thinking only about tomorrow. Again my thoughts went to my sisters.

I tried to conjure up some sense of longing for that life, but I didn't miss it. I missed my sisters, but not the farm. I felt like I'd been suffocating in a tiny closet, and now I was free, gasping in my fill of the cool, fresh, sweet air.

I wanted to stay free, if only for a little while longer.

Odin hoisted himself out of the hot tub and grabbed towels and fluffy white matching hotel bathrobes for the three of us to bundle up in. Minutes later, the food came.

The room service waiter was allowed to set the table properly this time, with a linen tablecloth and linen napkins and fine silver, all set out right over the same table where I'd been so evilly and deliciously spanked just an hour earlier.

Thor caught me staring and he smiled.

I narrowed my eyes and shook my head.

The three of us sat down to feast, wearing our matching fluffy robes. We ate and laughed. I drank a glass of champagne, which made me feel a little better about things.

"Doesn't get any better than this," Odin said.

"You guys wearing kilts would be better," I joked, but it wasn't really a joke.

Odin gave me a dark look. "Don't hold your breath."

I sighed. "I really do need to get a message to my sisters."

"We'll talk to Zeus," Thor said.

I finished my entire plate of pasta plus half my pizza before I threw in the napkin.

Odin sat back in his chair, one arm sprawled over the chair beside him, feeding himself chocolate-covered cherries.

"I see chocolate-covered cherries as really 1970s," I said.

"Am I going to have to punish you again?" Odin asked.

"You said to always be honest."

Odin grunted.

Thor turned his chair and set his feet on my lap. "I see them more as a 1960s food. But you sure get more chocolate bang for your buck than with chocolate-covered strawberries."

Odin picked up one of the champagne bottles and drank straight from it, completely draining it. I drained my flute and Thor poured more from the other bottle.

Eventually I ended up on Odin's lap with Thor's feet on my lap, and us feasting on dessert like decadent Roman gods. We even called down for more champagne.

"Is there a vomitorium in this place?" I asked. "One more chocolate and I'm there."

Odin and Thor laughed. I was so glad they got the reference. These guys were weirdly well educated. Or else they read a lot, like I did. You do that when you're stuck on a sheep farm.

"What about Zeus?" I asked. "I mean, he's been working out all this time?"

"He can go two, three hours."

"So...he should be back soon, right? Should we have waited for him? To eat with us?"

Thor shrugged. "He's a big boy."

"Let him be," Odin said darkly.

I rubbed my finger along the rim of the glass. "Does he ever join in, you know..."

The two of them glanced at each other.

"You know what I mean," I said.

"The bank robberies?" Thor asked.

I pinched one of his toes. "No. You know what I mean. The reindeer games."

Odin put his hands around my belly. "Did you just call them reindeer games?"

"Does he?" I pressed. "Does he join in ever?"

They exchanged glances and said nothing.

"Excuse my curiosity, having just been with two men for the first ever time and wanting to know if another will be added. Color me curious."

"You don't get to be curious about things," Odin said.

"Come on." I looked over at Thor. "Isis wants to know."

Thor swirled the champagne in his glass and stared out the window. "Do you *want* him to join in?"

"Do you?" I asked.

"Yes," Thor said. "We always do. It would be good. It would mean..." He paused, rephrased. "It would have a positive meaning."

"It's not likely, though," Odin added. "Very unlikely at this point."

A knock at the door. "Room service."

Odin exchanged glances with Thor. "Enter," he called.

A new room service waiter entered with a bucket of ice and our new bottle of champagne.

Odin smiled, ejecting me from his lap—roughly, I thought. "Please. And take the empty."

Thor sprang up. "Awesome!"

Odin collected some of our discarded clothes as the waiter popped the cork. He was a big guy with splotchy skin. "May I?"

"Sure." I pushed my glass to the center of the table, watching the bubbles dance in the golden liquid as he poured. I brought the glass to my lips.

"Don't drink it," Thor said.

I looked up. Thor stood behind the waiter, holding a gun to his ribs. I widened my eyes.

What was happening? Did they not like the service? Usually that would be reflected in the tip.

Odin ripped a piece of duct tape from a roll and slapped it over the man's mouth, then yanked a gun from the man's pocket and set it on the table.

Thor pulled out his wallet, handling the man roughly.

Odin yanked the man's head back by his hair. "How many out there?"

The man mumbled frantically under the tape, eye's rabid and wild.

"What's going on?" I couldn't believe the change in Odin and Thor, as if they'd transformed into dangerous militants.

Thor searched through the man's wallet and extracted an ID. "Always so convenient to know where a man lives. On account of the propensity to give wrong information."

Odin jerked the man by the hair again. "Fingers. How many?"

I backed up.

"Fine." Thor walked over and opened the sliding door to the balcony. The night sounds burst in the window on a rush of cool air. "Off you go. One." A pause. "Two."

The man held up his hands.

"Where?"

The man mumbled.

"Fuck up and we'll waste you right here." Odin ripped the tape from his mouth.

"Seven in the hall, two at each exit," the man blurted. "You can still walk out of here. Get Barzun. We can negotiate."

"Fucking-g negotiations." Odin practically spat the word. "Fuck them."

The waiter addressed me. "I don't know where you came from, but I know you're not part of this. You can help yourself. These guys won't help you, but you make this go—"

"Enough." Odin grabbed the champagne bottle and squeezed the man's cheeks together. "Drink." He poured champagne into his mouth. The man spat and struggled.

"Now." Thor shoved the gun into the man's temple and the man started glugging and then he coughed. Odin clapped a hand over the man's mouth, forcing him to swallow, and then they force-fed him some more.

I pulled my bathrobe tight around me. The man stumbled back, seeming to lose his balance, and then he just collapsed onto the floor. Thor knelt beside him and pulled open one of the man's eyelids. "Strong stuff," he said.

Odin duct taped the man's mouth and hands and dragged him off.

"What's going on?" I asked. "Did they follow us here?"

"This isn't from the robbery." Thor pulled on his pants. "It's from something else. Get your clothes on."

"Are they cops?"

"Nope," Thor said simply.

I dressed with shaking hands. "Seven guys in the hall? What are you going to do? He said you can still walk out of here."

"He was lying, Isis." Thor snapped a fanny pack around his waist. "They'd never let us walk out of here. We wouldn't make it to the elevator."

"But they're from the government?"

"In a manner of speaking," Odin said, tossing a rope out the balcony, attaching part to the wrought iron railing.

"We're going over?"

"No, we're going up. Come on." Thor pulled me down a hall, down into the far bathroom and started pulling off ceiling panels until he got to a locked hatch.

Odin climbed up onto the side of the tub and worked at a lock with some tiny tools that looked like dental instruments.

Thor set a hand on my shoulder. "We're going to leave you up on the roof and you'll stay there. You'll be safe there. They don't even know you exist right now. The recon man was surprised by your presence. Did you see that, Odin?"

Odin grunted his agreement.

"He expected three guys, but he got two guys and a girl. Plus, he'll be out for a day."

"But the first room service waiter saw me."

Thor shook his head. "That one was a real waiter. They keep their noses down. Plus, we gave him two fifties."

Odin shoved open the hatch.

"What about you guys?" I asked.

"Up." Thor made a step with his hands.

I took off my heels, strapped them around my wrist, and scrambled up into the dark space above the ceiling after Odin.

"Sub-roof," Odin whispered.

The place hummed with fans and machines. The rough concrete floor was cold on my bare feet, and the ceiling was so low, we had to crouch. It was like a workshop for mechanically inclined gnomes.

Thor hoisted himself up.

He and Odin took great care to replace everything from above, making the bathroom ceiling look as normal as possible, I guessed.

All the better to make people think they'd gone over the side.

We climbed up a ladder through a ceiling door and emerged on the dark rooftop in a forest of mammoth metal fans and blowers of different shapes and sizes.

The roof was covered with a black semi-spongy substance that felt warm under my feet.

Wind whipped my hair. My heart pounded like a bongo.

I felt like we'd stepped onto the edge of the world.

Odin pulled a phone from his pack and made a call, then he shook his head Thor. "Voicemail."

Thor grumbled.

"Hey, Z, get out and get to the car now. We're up top. Visitors. Call us, dammit!" Odin stuffed his phone back in the pack. "They thought he was in the suite. You heard."

"They thought he was there," Thor confirmed. "Definitely."

Odin got up and moved away from us, walking bent over like he was in a war zone, careful footsteps across the dark roof.

"What's happening?" I asked breathlessly.

"A lot of highly trained guys are down there, and they're looking for us. I'm sorry we brought you into this."

"It's okay—"

"Listen—we forced you up here, okay?" He clutched my shoulders. "We terrorized you, cut your hair, kept you drugged, got it? Act catatonic and too upset to talk about anything. If they've hooked you up with the stunt you pulled in the traffic jam, there was a gun on you. Okay? But don't volunteer it. Act traumatized and silent. Repeat after me, 'I can act traumatized and silent for as long as I goddamn want.'"

I stared at him, confused. "What about you?"

He shook me. "Say it!"

"I can act silent and traumatized as long as I goddamn want."

"Months if I want. They can't fuck with me if I don't talk."

"They can't fuck with me if I don't talk," I repeated. "Don't worry. But what about you?"

"We'll find Zeus. Get to the van. Try not to make a hot exit."

"I can still be your hostage," I said. "Wouldn't that help?"

"It only helps if they want the hostage to stay alive. These aren't cops, remember?"

"They wouldn't care if I got killed?"

"They'd prefer it," Thor said. "Witnesses tend to complicate things."

My blood raced. Everything seemed surreal. This wasn't a game any longer.

Chapter Ten

"Is Zeus is still in the workout room?" I asked, wrapping my arms around myself, gazing out over the rooftop panorama beyond the hotel, darkness interspersed with car lights and buildings with lit windows.

"Yeah," Thor said. "But he's not answering. Which means he's heavy into his workout or he's got trouble. But the recon guy seemed to think he was in our suite so...look, we just don't know. We can't let him go up to the suite, that's all. We have to get down there and warn him."

"You can't go back in!" I said.

"We won't leave without Zeus. It's not how we do things. We don't leave each other behind."

"No matter what?" I asked.

"No matter what."

Meaning they'd die before they'd leave each other. Shivers came over me—primal shivers—the kind you get when you glimpse something majestically bigger than yourself. It's here I think I fell in love with them. Not individually, but the gang itself and their fierce loyalty to each other.

Odin was back. "Maybe drop into a room on the east?"

Thor sighed.

Odin tried another call again. "*Fucking-g answer!*" he whisper-yelled at the phone.

"You can't go back inside and get him without risk, but what if I did?" I asked. "You just need to warn Zeus, right?"

Thor shook his head.

"You said they don't know me. They're watching for you, not me. For all they know, I'm a hotel guest. I can't pop down to the workout room?"

"Pop down how? No," Thor said.

"It's not like I have anything at stake."

Odin pulled out his phone and stared at it. "If we hadn't split up, we'd be on the highway."

"They're probably in the room by now, aren't they?" I said. "These guys wanting to kill you. And then they'll start searching the hotel." And apparently, they didn't mind about killing hostages. Oh, I didn't like these guys.

"They're not in the room yet," Odin said mysteriously. Lord knows how he knew. My guys were masters of knowing things—dirty and otherwise.

I got up and scurried across the roof to the other side, just as Odin had, and looked over. You could see balconies below—the top-floor balconies were maybe ten feet down. And far beyond was the pool. Tiny people swam and drank under lights, unaware of the drama above. I wanted to do something to help my guys.

In my mind, at least, they were my guys now.

Thor caught up. "What the fuck are you doing?"

"You could lower me, right? To that balcony? People never lock their balcony doors. I saw that on TV. I'd just walk through and take the elevator down. You said nobody knows who I am. This would be easy. *For me.*"

"What if somebody's in the room?" Odin asked, watching my eyes.

"I'll look, and if there're people, I'll go to the next one."

"It's a long way down to be swinging between balconies," Thor said.

"Are you being sexist? The girl can't do it? I've rock climbed. I've bungee and ski jumped. I'm already there. Just lower me. Seriously, I can't walk through the hotel? No—I can. *You* guys can't, but *I* can. I'm Isis, bitches!"

Odin scowled.

"Still," Thor said.

"I'll be the messenger. But it won't be free, of course. You'll owe me. I'll want something in exchange."

This got their attention. I'd noticed that they were more apt to take me up on things when I demanded something in return, locked them into a bargain. This was a group that operated, in a strange way, on consensual bargaining.

"What's the favor?" Odin asked.

"It'll cost you twenty thousand dollars."

"We have that." Odin exchanged glances with Thor. Something passed between them. "Let him freak," Odin said, even though Thor had said nothing. "Let him."

Zeus, he meant.

Thor closed his eyes. So, if I started participating like this, it would upset Zeus? But I could do it so easily! This was nothing compared to the ski jump.

I put my hand on the edge—black tar, still warm from the day. "Who has the van keys? How will you get to the van?"

"Just get the message to him. We'll handle the van." Odin held a phone out. "Star two is Thor. If you get to him and see that he's in trouble, keep walking to the pool door and prop it open, then call us and describe the trouble."

Thor hissed out a breath.

"She volunteered," Odin snapped. "She's a big girl. It's not a hard task for somebody not afraid of heights. Ice, you just get to the workout room and tip off Zeus." He told me where it was as he pulled a coiled wire out of his pack, hooked one end to something, and handed me a pair of gloves.

Thor gave him a look.

"We'll share your gloves," Odin said.

He turned to me. "Go two floors down, not the top. It'll be safer. Can you do that?"

"Sure."

Thor said, "You're sure?"

"I'm thrilled, frankly." In fact, I was greatly enjoying the feeling of being up on top of the ski jump, about to get exhilarated. I put on the gloves and made sure my strappy shoes were secured around my wrists. "Once I'm inside, should I take the elevator?"

"Definitely," Odin said. "Be normal. And if you can't find him, assume we're gone and do whatever you need to do to look out for yourself."

I took hold of the wire and climbed over the side. The gloves gave me great traction—I hoped my guys would be okay with just one glove each. I slid down, pushing off the balcony and sliding on down to the next one. I hooked a leg over, then another, and then I was in, standing on the balcony below, feeling very Bond girl.

I crept to the sliding door and tried it, pleased to find it unlocked. The room was dark, which ideally meant it was empty, or else the occupants were sleeping, in which case they'd hopefully continue sleeping. I yanked the cord to show I was set, took a breath, opening the door all the way, and crept in.

Luck was with me—or else the low hotel occupancy rate was, because the room was indeed empty.

I walked to the door, slipped on my high heels, and walked

down the hall with poise, smiling sunnily at a trio of businessy-looking people who were passing the other way.

Nothing to see here! Just a hotel guest doing hotel-guest things!

They just gave me weird looks, which I thought was a bit rude. But then I stepped into the elevator and saw in the mirror panel how dirty I had gotten on the roof. There was even a nearly theatrical smudge of grime on my face.

Well...maybe the cast of *Les Miserables* was in town. Did they ever think of that?

I stabbed the LL button and brushed and straightened myself best I could as I studied the map on the elevator wall, which showed that the exercise room was two rights and a left from the elevator bank.

What did this map also show? That the hotel was designed by somebody obsessed with mazes.

After what felt like the slowest elevator ride on the planet, the door opened and I rushed out past the pool area, down a small hallway, and burst into the exercise room.

And froze when I saw the three bodies slumped in the corner.

Dead?

And where was Zeus?

Somebody grabbed me from behind and clapped a hand over my mouth.

I froze.

A man's voice. "Shh. It's me."

Zeus.

He let go and I spun around. "Odin and Thor are up on the roof!" I held out the phone for him. "Star two for Thor."

"What are you doing?" he demanded.

"Getting you a message from Thor and Odin."

"No, no, you can't. No." He grabbed the phone from me, grumbling.

You're welcome, I thought as Zeus stabbed the buttons and proceeded to have a mysterious and angry conversation, all o'clocks and coordinates, his keen green gaze knifing through me all the while. I tried not to stare at the bodies, which wasn't easy. Dead bodies tend to be a focal point in any room.

He spun around and walked to the window, still talking, staring out over the indoor pool on the other side of the glass, water lit dreamily by underwater lights. It was here that I noticed his arm and shoulder covered in blood.

What are you doing? He'd barked. Maybe it wasn't the worst question ever. What *was* I doing?

From the clipped conversation, I got that he had been just about to steal upstairs to warn Thor and Odin. None of these guys would leave without the others. A phone lay broken on the floor.

It was here I felt something cold on my neck. I stiffened in fright as a hand grabbed my hair. "You move and you bleed."

A haze descended over me.

So the guys on the floor weren't dead.

Zeus turned, looking annoyed, like we were interrupting his call. "Later," he said.

"Drop the phone," the man said to Zeus, holding me in front of him, knife to my throat. I tried not to panic, not to move, not even to swallow.

The blade bit in.

The room seemed too bright.

Zeus smiled coldly. Instead of dropping the phone, he took a few steps toward me, and casually raised a gun and pressed it to my forehead.

I gasped.

"She moves and she bleeds?" Zeus said. "Okay. And so do you."

I felt like I was seeing the scene from outside my own body, everything slow, surreal.

"I mean it," the man said.

"You guys still using tungsten shot?" Zeus continued. "My guess is yes, and that this bullet from your friend's piece will pierce clear through her skull and right into your jugular. Shall we test it?"

My knees went liquid. The tick of the wall clock became deafening.

Zeus's eyes were cold on mine. "How long have we known each other, honey?"

"Uh…" I couldn't think. A day? No, less…

"Go ahead, tell the man the truth."

"S-since this morning. Around eleven."

Zeus sighed. "Hopefully my partners gave you a satisfying sendoff. I *am* sorry about this."

"What?" I gasped.

He winced, as if preparing to shoot me. *Expecting spatter*, I realized with horror.

"No!" I cried.

The man shoved me. The knife was off my throat and he was backing away, moving behind a workout machine, apparently deciding stacks of metal weights were more bulletproof than my skull.

I put my hand over the place the knife had bit in. Blood, but not much.

Zeus stalked toward the guy and followed him around and around the largest weights machine. The man kept going in circles until Zeus simply pushed the thing over, crashing it sideways. Then he jumped over it and kicked the guy in the face.

Literally in the face.

I'd never seen anything so bluntly violent. It was nothing like a karate kick—no jumps or spins, just Zeus's foot coming out of nowhere and snapping viciously up into the man's face. The man convulsed on his feet and then simply crumpled down on top of the machine and rolled onto the floor.

I covered my open mouth with my hand.

Zeus whipped a towel over his shoulders to hide his bloody arm.

"Thank you," I breathed. *I guess.*

"Thank you?" Zeus came toward me now, eyes dark and ferocious. "I would've just as easily killed you. I would've done it in a heartbeat—don't you ever doubt it."

"What?"

"I do what I need to do to protect the group, and that doesn't include you. I know you're having fun playing bank robbers right now, but that's something you need to understand. You're not in the group."

"I was delivering a message, not trying to join your group."

Zeus shoved the gun and the phone in his sweatpants pocket. "We gotta get out of here."

He stalked out through the pool area.

I followed him. through a series of doors and then out into the cool, starry night. I touched my neck. It wasn't bleeding as much.

Pop-pop-pops like firecrackers sounded out in the distance.

"Yahoos breached the room," he mumbled as we hurried across the parking lot to the van. "Get in the back."

I jumped in and closed the door. He started up the van and drove. Slowly. Meanderingly, even. In this way, he made the van itself a disguise.

I marveled at the extreme discipline it would take to drive so listlessly instead of frantically racing across the lot, which would've been my move. I mean, killers were after them. Thor and Odin, presumably, were waiting somewhere.

"...that doesn't make you part of the group," Zeus had said. His words stung, but they confirmed so much about these guys. That they had survived against dangerous enemies with a fierce, almost

wolf-pack-like loyalty, sacrificing outsiders and even their own safety for each other.

A wolf pack thing—or a God Pack thing. And he'd made it painfully clear that I was the outsider.

I wished I was inside.

Zeus rounded the side of the hotel and slowed near a thicket of bushes that hugged the corner of the hotel. Thor and Odin burst out, piled in, and we were off.

"Denko," Zeus said to Odin, who was riding up front as usual. "Had to be."

Odin nodded. "Denko."

Zeus pulled onto the main thoroughfare and drove at the speed limit.

Thor scooted over. "Are you okay?"

"Yes," I whispered. A lie. I was scared. Trembling.

He inspected my neck, palpating the skin around it. "What happened?"

Zeus said, "Down in the weight room one of the ops tried to hold Isis. We convinced him she was nobody, though."

"I think it was made clear, yes," I said.

"He tried to hold you?" Thor said.

"So I threatened to shoot them both," Zeus said, like it was nothing.

"Through my *skull*," I added. "A two-for-one." I felt proud of myself for speaking of it so casually. I felt Odin's eyes on me.

"Mess with the bull, you get the horns," Zeus growled.

Did he mean the guy he'd kicked in the face? Or did he mean me?

"Zeus, you need medical attention," Thor said to him sternly.

"Let's put down some distance first," Zeus said.

Thor turned to me then, and he put out his hand, palm up. I rested my hand in his and he closed his fingers around mine and just held my hand, there in the back seat, careening through the darkness.

Such a simple gesture, but at that moment, it meant everything.

I knew I was an outsider—Zeus had made that clear—but right then and there, Thor let me in a little.

Chapter Eleven

THE GUYS DROVE THROUGH THE NIGHT, TAKING TURNS, stopping once for burgers and once for medical supplies.

We switched off seats after that. I was allowed to ride in front, and Thor got in back with Zeus.

There was a lot of grunting, and then Thor grumbled something that sounded like "*slug in there*" and I realized he was digging an actual bullet out of Zeus's arm.

Right in the back seat!

I don't know if I was more shocked Zeus had a bullet in his arm the whole time, or that Thor was digging it out.

"Odin!" I said, tipping my head at the back seat. You could see the weariness in Odin's eyes; he was too tired to be driving.

"Don't worry, Thor's a doctor."

"A doctor?"

"That's right," Odin said. "What's so weird about that?"

"You just don't see that many bank-robber-doctors."

Plus, he seemed to be the least responsible of the three of them. The others were all into keeping him in line, it seemed.

These guys didn't add up. Thor, a doctor.

What was Odin?

What was Zeus?

There was some gutter dog in Zeus, that's for sure. I didn't know if I'd ever get over the feeling of his gun at my forehead. Or the way he stalked that guy, then delivered that weirdly vicious kick. *I would've just as easily killed you. I would've done it in a heartbeat—don't you ever doubt it.*

I'd heard darkness in Zeus's words.

Zeus was a force, like a storm: frightening and magnificent, with a charged power churning inside. Maybe I should've been angry at him for being all, *would've just as easily killed you*, but you don't get mad at a storm for blowing things over.

Or ripping up flowers.

I asked about the room service waiter and the man in the workout room. What if they recognized me and put them together with the bank job?

The guys thought that was funny. "These operatives don't give a fuck about any bank. It's under their radar. Banks are not their concern."

"Then what is their concern? Who are they? Why are they after you?"

Zeus said, "One more question like that and you're on the side of the road, deal or no deal."

"We actually have two deals now, I believe."

"Two?"

"That's right," I said. Zeus was none too pleased to hear about the price I'd demanded for my messenger services. But I didn't care. It made me feel like I was part of things.

At around two in the morning, we crashed in a roadside motel in Missouri, just outside Kansas City. Thor and I bunked in one room and Odin and Zeus in another, and sex was definitely not in the air—we were all dead on our feet. Thor didn't even wash up. He just collapsed on our king-sized bed. I brushed my teeth using my finger and Thor's toothpaste, and then I, too, collapsed, stretched out next to Thor under the cool, clean sheets.

I woke up in the early hours with Thor snuggled up to me, whispering something. Was he trying to wake me up?

"Thor?"

Thor whispered some more, a stream of nonsense. A bad dream, I realized. I couldn't make out most of the words. I got a lot of *nos* and *don'ts*, and out-of-context phrases like *don't leave Venus*. His sleeping face was a mask of pain.

Don't leave Venus? Was he having a bad dream about interplanetary travel?

"It's okay," I whispered. "We're safe. You're on Earth."

He squirmed and turned onto his back. I waited, but he said no more.

For all the guns and domination and violence, Thor had a little Peter Pan in him.

All three of them did.

They were running, these guys, but I couldn't shake the feeling that they'd been abandoned, too.

Lost.

Bereft.

My badass Peter Pans.

I touched Thor's hair. I liked the notion that maybe I'd calmed him in his nightmare. Like I'd helped.

These guys scared me a little, but I envied their love, their loyalty, their bravery.

Here I was in a shitty motel with a headache and no toothbrush, lying next to a doctor-turned-bank-robber who was also a sex maniac who carried a gun, and a fugitive on some scary wanted list. And I was feeling slightly sore from fucking him and another guy at the same time and emotionally exhausted from almost being killed.

And I wanted nothing more than to stay.

Was that wrong?

I desperately wanted it. I felt like everything in my past was pointing to this place, to these men.

To this life.

I wanted this life with every cell in my body.

I felt like I was home.

My mind floated back to my sisters. Had they slept? Were they freaking out? I've always protected them. That would never change. I needed them to know that I was okay.

I'd brought up the topic of contacting them on the road last night.

Later, Zeus had said.

Thor flopped back over onto his other side, but I still couldn't sleep. I wandered into the bathroom and looked in the mirror. My hair—now there was something to freak out about. I looked like a demented redheaded Dutch boy.

Some time later, I woke up to the scent of coffee and the sounds of Thor packing stuff up. He'd slicked down his curls and had put on a brown sports jacket and jeans and boots, a get-up that made him look more like a movie director than yesterday's slick businessman.

When I commented on his new look, he pulled out mirrored aviator glasses and put them on, which made him look shockingly hot.

"You have as many looks as a Ken doll," I teased.

He came to the bed and put his hands on either side of me. He leaned down close, still wearing the sunglasses, looking very serious, now. "But I have one look a Ken doll never has."

What did he mean by that? What look does a Ken doll never have?

Then my face turned red.

He grinned, looming over me, all dressed up and spiffy compared to my scantily clad self. I liked it.

Goose bumps rode up my skin as he touched my throat and traced a line down to center of my chest. "Do you know what Odin said about you?"

"What?" Electricity skittered wherever his finger touched. He drew it down, down toward my belly.

"Odin says a frisson of vulnerability turns you on. I'm inclined to agree."

"Oh, yeah? Is Odin a psychoanalyst from Vienna now?"

"Let's just say Odin has your number. Odin has everybody's number." Thor stood. "Unfortunately, we have to go. We have a lot to do."

So we were all business then. I got up and put on my shabby bank teller outfit.

We took a cab to downtown Kansas City. Luckily, our first stop was an upscale department store where I picked out a trio of lovely sundresses and some awesome tops and pants, the sorts of things Isis might wear. And then we went to a beauty salon on what Thor termed "the rock 'n' roll side of town" for new hair.

I took the chair in front of a purple-haired stylist who curled her heavily pierced lip in horror as she inspected my knife-chopped locks. "It was definitely a hasty job," I said "But I want a big change anyway. Can we make it short and pink?"

"Hold on," Thor said. "Pink?" He shook his head.

"She should have the style she chooses," the stylist snapped. "You want pink? Pink would be gorgeous on you."

"But if she looks too radical or out of the ordinary," Thor said, "she could lose the very important position she currently has. She might cease to be effective in her profession. Which has a public interaction component."

"He's right," I said. "How about jet-black?"

Thor shook his head.

"Dark brown," I said.

This, too, Thor vetoed.

"What?" I protested.

"Come here."

"One minute," I said to the stylist. I took off the plastic poncho she'd put on me and followed Thor out onto the sidewalk, glaring at his back the whole way.

"You can't have your hair short and dark."

"Why? It'll look totally natural."

He took off his sunglasses and eyed me straight on. "No go."

"Why not? I can't have it red. So that leaves blonde. It's blonde or nothing? Is that the deal here?"

"Yeah. Trust me." The gravity in his voice suggested a world of pain, of trouble.

Slowly things assembled themselves in the back of my mind... the hole, the rules. And the way I fit in, at least with Thor and Odin, almost like there was a place for me.

The sense of a ghost.

"Because that's how she had it," I whispered. "Short, dark hair."

He cocked his head, as though confused, but I suspected he understood.

And then it came to me. *Don't leave Venus.* Except he wasn't giving instructions for space travel.

"Venus," I added.

He caged me against the wall. "None of us told you that."

"You told me! You said it in your sleep. *Don't leave, Venus,* you said."

His frown deepened.

"I can tell there was a girl before," I said softly.

He sighed. "Congratulations. Now you know why you can't make it brown."

I felt bad, like I'd betrayed him by figuring out his sleep talk. "Sorry," I said.

He put his hand around the back of his neck and stared up at the sky. I waited, noticing he had freckles across his nose, so light they were almost translucent.

What in the world had happened to Venus?

"Tell me," I said.

He took his hand from his neck and looked at me then, lashes pale in the morning sun, contrasting with the rich blue of his eyes. I said nothing more. Thor was the sensitive one, the communicative one, the one who got out of line most easily. I felt like if I gave him space, he'd fill it with information.

And then he did.

"She's the reason you can't stay," he said.

"But I *want* to stay." I couldn't believe I'd said it aloud.

He squinted into the sunlight; I suspected the squint was more to cover up happiness than to protect his eyes. "Your sisters—"

"I can help them from afar. People my age leave home all the time. I'll figure it out."

"You don't know what you're saying. You don't know what this is."

"I know enough of it to know I love it. I love this whole thing."

"You've been with us a day."

"Sometimes, Thor, people just *know things*. Sometimes in life you make a big decision because you *know*. Haven't you ever done that?"

The way he looked at me, I knew that he had. That he understood. "I want you to stay. I want you to. I can tell that Odin does, too."

My pulse raced. Could this actually happen? "Two against one?"

He smiled bitterly. "Aren't you observant. But keeping you with us is not something for a vote. It's something we all have to agree on. The thing is, I'm telling you this in confidence. I'm telling you because..." he gazed into the middle distance. "I don't know why I'm telling you."

"Okay."

Thor smoothed back his hair. "The thing with Venus is that it was only supposed to be a sex thing. We met her at a hotel bar and let her think we were traveling on business, and we made up those rules, you know, if she wanted to travel with us, she'd obey these rules." He paused as a couple passed. "They're the rules we told you. She'd just been fired, we were flush, and so it was all fun and games. And then she helped us out in a pinch. Does that sound familiar to you?"

"Yes," I said, recalling the rooftop glance between Odin and Thor.

"It was good. But then we relied on her to do another thing and she got some heat on her—just cops, but still, it tied her to a robbery, and suddenly she couldn't go home again. Not ever. And she had family. She said she was fine, but she hadn't chosen it. She was stuck with us, but her heart wasn't in it. She wasn't cut out for it."

He paused, watched a man unload boxes from the back of a truck and stack them outside the Vietnamese grocery across the street.

"She even drove for us sometimes. Then she made a careless mistake that brought a lot of heat down on us. There's a line you cross in this game where you want to be caught a little bit, just for the intensity to ease. Consciously you don't, but subconsciously, you get tired."

I nodded.

"She crossed that line," he continued. "We quit bringing her along anywhere having to do with the jobs, just brought her along to hotels or kept her in the hideouts. That was the beginning of the end. Zeus thinks we broke her. I don't know. We sure didn't help her."

"I'm sorry."

"I'm not talking against her. She was beautiful." He looked at me hard, wanting me to get that. "She was a beautiful person. She held us together. She connected us. Changed us inside. Reconfigured us—even Zeus. Venus was a little wrong, but we loved her."

"Sounds like."

"So one day, after all the trouble, we find this lipstick message on the dash of the Camaro we'd been driving around—*You're better off without me*. We looked for her. Especially Zeus."

I held my breath, waiting for him to continue.

"Some workers in a quarry pit found her body. She'd gone and jumped off a cliff, basically."

"I'm so sorry."

"Zeus felt responsible," Thor continued. "He'd been hard on her, and things were getting messed up at the end. Twisted. Zeus can get very intense."

I thought about the blunt violence in Zeus's kick. The surprise of it, like he knew every way to go at a man, including the unexpected ones.

"He has deep emotions and not a lot of impulse control, let's just say. He asked her to do things he shouldn't have asked."

I was surprised Thor had told me so much.

A man in a white apron came out of the grocery across the street, stacking boxes.

"It's not enough that you want to stay with us. Or that Odin and I might want you to. Here's the thing—it's been a year almost, and...you just throwing in with us, it's hard on Zeus. He feels responsible for what happened with Venus, grieved her the most. It wasn't his fault—none of us understood her state of mind—but he takes it on himself. He gets fierce about people, and the way we live right now, a year is like a decade. Everything's bigger. The danger, the rewards, the fear, the pleasure. And we pulled Venus in so fast and furious, and we got very symbiotic with her. When she died, it damaged us in a lot of ways you wouldn't expect. Zeus particularly."

I thought about the flowers, of course. But I thought about what Thor wasn't saying. Last night I'd heard the pain in his voice loud and clear. *Don't. No. Don't leave, Venus.*

"I'm sorry," I said again.

"That's why we can't keep you."

"I'm not a stray puppy. I'm not Venus."

"Then don't get your hair brown." His words were part command, part collaboration. Did Venus have brown hair?

It was a sprig of hope, at any rate. "Blonde it is."

I went in and told the stylist to cut my hair short and to color it platinum blonde. Thor went off to do some mysterious errands.

"You're sure you don't want dark? It's your hair," she said.

"Absolutely."

She clearly didn't approve. She thought I was being ruled, oppressed. She couldn't know that for the first time in my life I was truly free—dizzyingly free—and that my number-one wish was to stay this way.

I mused on what Thor had said. The loss they couldn't quite heal from. My poor badass Peter Pans, all alone in the world.

Thor picked me up a couple of hours later—literally. He walked into the salon where I'd just paid—with the money they'd stolen from FCN bank—and hoisted me up in his arms and twirled me around and kissed me. "You are so beautiful."

I laughed. "Thanks, boss."

And then it was time for the message to my sisters. We had it all worked out.

We cabbed to the nice side of town, to an upscale bath and linens shop, one of a small, exclusive chain that had ordered our quilts before.

He grabbed my hand as we walked in. With my new dress and haircut and his whole Hollywood look, I suppose we seemed quite the power couple. We pretended to browse the quilt selection.

A shop girl came to help us. Nothing we saw would do.

"I'm looking for a non-toxic organic sheep's wool comforter," I said. "In king. Do you have anything like that? Or can you get anything like that?"

Ten minutes later we were at the checkout desk with the manager eyeing her computer, clicking around.

"I don't care what it costs," I said. "I want the best, top of the line."

"Mmm. One of our vendors has a pretty pricey one. With handling, you're looking at twenty-two thousand dollars." She peered up, expression neutral.

A markup of two thousand. I smiled. "Is it organic domestic sheep's wool?"

"Yes, and very high quality. This is a high-quality vendor. Our Atlanta store has worked with them. The Paris Hilton comforter. Comes in cream or eggshell only."

They were actually the same color. When I'd made the site, I'd wanted to give people the illusion of choice. "I'll take eggshell."

She furrowed her brow. "Now, here's the thing—it's non-returnable. I'd have to have you pay up front. We'd call when it's ready. Six to eight weeks." She looked up. Such an exorbitant price. I wondered if she was secretly freaking out.

"Do you take American Express?" Thor and I had made sure they didn't. We had the cash to pay for it, but it would look weird to whip it out right off.

She shook her head.

Thor rolled his eyes. "Fine. We're going to the bank today. We'll come back and just pay in cash. Is that okay? You take cash, right?"

"Of course," she said.

Thor was good at playing the privileged snot. It made me wonder about his past. Who *were* these guys?

<h1 style="text-align:center">Chapter Twelve</h1>

We walked out and went down the street to a posh café with a secluded porch in the back. I got spaghetti with obscene amounts of cheese grated onto it. Thor got fish. The doctor, eating healthy. I teased him about it, and he responded in his sexy-warning way, legs tangling with mine.

Fun fact: food tastes way better when it's bought with money stolen from a guy like Hank Vernon.

Thor called Odin and Zeus on his new throwaway phone—the two other members of our God Pack were out buying a used vehicle and working out something with the diamonds. They were to pick us up after the comforter buy.

Thor had a clipped conversation where he looked at me a lot. When he hung up, he informed me that Zeus had planned out our next job already, for a First City National in a suburb of Omaha. They'd go for it after just two days of surveillance.

"It was supposed to take a week," I said.

"It was," Thor said. "The timetable's sped up."

"What does that mean?"

"What do you think it means?"

"That Zeus wants me gone."

Thor swirled his lemonade around in the wine glass it had come in. "I think Odin will be proud of what we've accomplished today. I particularly think he'll enjoy your hair," he said, attempting a subject change.

I broke a breadstick, ate half. He didn't want to say more. I could respect that.

"And I mean that in the most unwholesome way you could possibly ever take it."

I stopped eating. "What?"

"The *most* unwholesome way."

I narrowed my eyes. "Are you telling me Odin will mess up my salon blowout?"

He reached across our little table and touched my hair, like he had a right to. And he did, according to the notorious rules. "Thoroughly."

He was using that rough silky-rumbly voice of his that I loved.

I slid the other half of my breadstick into my mouth, eyeing him.

His expression turned playful. "I'm only telling you because there are things—" here he lowered his voice— "things you need to be ready for. Things you need to think about during our five-hour journey coming up. So that you can be prepared to obey us once we reach our destination."

My stomach tightened. "Is that so?"

"That is exactly so." He went on to tell me some of those things in his roughly caressing tone, lowering his voice to a grumbly whisper when anybody came near.

I shifted in my seat as he described how they might position my legs. How they might restrain my arms. What my breasts would look like when my arms were totally bound together at my back.

His words seemed to wind invisible tendrils around my thighs and my arms, pinning me to my seat, touching me under my clothes.

Heat bloomed inside me.

The man was a bit wild, but he understood his own power. And so did I.

"I won't tell you some of the other things we might do, because with certain activities, you just have to be there, don't you think? Some activities that seem unpleasant in the telling can be quite enjoyable in the doing."

"I suppose."

"You *suppose*," Thor grated out.

Three men entered the sunny porch dining area and sat down two tables away. He positioned his mirrored glasses back over his eyes, concealing his gaze, all the better to monitor them.

"I know how you enjoy being told things ahead of time," he added, "but some are best without warning."

Gulp.

He went back onto the subject of my hair. Which would be so messed up.

I didn't exactly love the idea of getting it messed up after the stylist got it to look so nice, but I was sure the journey of getting it messed up would be worth it.

Back at the haute bath and linen shop, we paid the woman in hundreds.

I acted excited about my new comforter. "Is there a way to send a message along with my order? I assume it's custom made."

I'd discussed this move with the guys. I'd assured them that my sister Vanessa handled the orders, and that she was a bright, devious, twenty-three-year-old woman who would understand the message and not take it to the cops. And even if she did, we'd be long gone from the store.

"They don't take special requests," she said.

"I just want to say something fun to them. To the artisans who make it." I happened to know there was a space where you could write a message, considering I'd built the site myself. "Can't you pass along a message? I buy many fine things from artisans, and I feel that if they know you are human and appreciative of their craft, they do an extra good job. Surely for twenty-two thousand—"

She held up a hand. "Of course. I don't see why I can't include a message with the order. What do you want to say?" She snapped the cash drawer shut.

"The customer ordering this wants you to know she's excited for her organic comforter, and—"

"Hold on, hold on," the woman said. She turned the monitor and started typing.

I repeated, "The customer ordering this wants you to know she's excited for her organic comforter, and maybe someday Paris Hilton will buy one for each room in her house, plus one for her dog, but in the meantime, it's going to a good home. A very happy home."

The woman gave me a too-long stare when I was done. "Well, that's...sweet," she said, but you could tell she really meant *insane.* Because who sends a message about Paris Hilton's dog? She took down my number and gave me her card.

I went out of there feeling lighter. Happier. My sister would know it was me. She would understand I was okay.

We waited at the appointed corner.

Zeus and Odin pulled up in a minivan, rocking out—in terms of both music and clothes, all black boots and plaid shirts, looking way less respectable than Thor and me. We got into the back seat.

Odin turned, watched me levelly. He liked the sundress and my hair, I could tell. The sundress was blood red, and laced up the front in a crisscross way, like tall boots. With that and my new bright crown of platinum, I felt as though I'd fully transformed into Isis. Zeus, of course, had merely flicked his eyes at me as I'd gotten in, then fixed his frowning attention back on the road as he pulled out, all stern and bullish.

"Gods driving a minivan," I said. "What has the world come to?"

"Are you mocking the gods of bank robbery?" Odin asked me. "Could it be that I am hearing you mocking us?"

I tipped my head, gave a tiny shrug. Yes, I was mocking them.

Odin shook his head sadly. "Oh, dear."

Desire heated in my belly at those two little words.

"How'd it go?" Zeus asked.

"As planned." Thor ran through the details of our day, the things he'd seen around the beauty salon and the restaurant. It shocked me, just how closely he'd been monitoring our surroundings the entire time. Odin informed Thor the diamonds were a no go, whatever that meant.

"And they still don't know anything about the bank," Zeus said. "The cops held a press conference. Your sisters were there."

"Wait, what? How did they seem?"

"How do you think they seemed? Pretty fucking upset," Zeus said. I caught his accusing gaze in the mirror. "You're their sister. You were taken as a hostage. You *left*."

"I had to."

"In the moment we took you, sure, you had to. But don't act like you can't be back there now. This extra job with us is *your* game plan. You could say the word and call it off and be back there tonight."

"They'll have the message and the money now," I said. "They'll know I'm okay."

"A message and money," Zeus practically spat, "can never make up for a person."

His words were like a punch in the gut. "I had to leave," I said.

"There are other ways to support a farm."

"But this is how events happened," I snapped. I didn't know

how to make him understand how it felt. How I was dying back there.

"How events *happened*." Even through the rearview mirror, Zeus's gaze pierced into me. "Like you have no responsibility for it." He looked away with disdain. "How convenient." His disdain was sharp as a knife. Only Zeus could do that.

"Maybe it is convenient," I snapped. "Maybe I'm a horrible person."

"Maybe we can tone it down," Odin said.

"It's in your power to put it all back together again, that's my point," Zeus said. "You should watch the press conference. When we get to Omaha, you can watch it for yourself."

"That'll be constructive," Thor said.

"She needs to see," Zeus said.

"I *want* to see." I crossed my arms over my chest. It would rip me apart, but of course I had to see.

"She rode an opportunity." Thor crossed his long, lanky legs. "She's exploiting an opportunity. You want to act like we don't do that every fucking day of the week?"

Zeus's eyes burned into the rearview mirror. I refused to look away. We were officially in a stare-down.

He looked away.

Even with him looking away, though, something dark and angular was growing between us.

"Well, you'll be back soon," Zeus grumbled. "I was thinking we might be able to get away with just a day of surveillance. Just rip in and ride that bank."

"One day?" Odin barked. "Are you fucking kidding me?"

"We rip in, just clean out the front," Zeus said. "It'll still be a robbery. We have the diamonds, there's no reason to go deep on this one."

"If we're gonna do it, let's do it right," Thor said.

"That is doing it right," Zeus growled. "Best to shake up our pattern. This one's in an urban area, too. Getting out'll be a cakewalk."

"Why'd you pick my bank?" I asked. "If it's easier to escape in an urban area?"

"We heard it was lax," Zeus said. "Somebody else would've knocked it over if we hadn't."

"One day. You're whack," Odin said.

"Who's the expert here?" Zeus demanded. "It's my realm. Is it not my realm?"

"Let's survey and see," Odin said.

"No, let's *do*," Zeus growled.

Odin said, "Let's take this offline."

Meaning, don't fight about it in front of me.

Zeus wanted me gone. I hated it. Should I leave? For the good of the group. Was my presence making them fight? Making them take undue risks?

But how could I?

Chapter Thirteen

We spent many hours in the van listening to the audiobook Odin had picked out for the road—evidently my badass Peter Pans favored sci-fi tales. The fun space adventure story evened out the harsh edges.

We stopped at another lonely gas station where we picked out candy. I grabbed a Kit Kat and took it up to the counter.

A voice from behind me: "Hey."

Zeus.

My heart skipped a beat. I turned to find him scowling at me, standing a bit too near, using his intimidating bulk—unfairly, I thought. "What?"

He plucked the Kit Kat bar from my fingers and looked at the code on the back of it. "Come here." He went back to the chocolate area, and I followed. He put my candy bar back and picked one from the back of the display and examined the wrapper. "Gas candy can get really old." He handed it to me. "This one's fresher. Okay?" He said the *okay* like I was about to argue.

Was this an apology?

"Got it." I nodded slowly, like he was a wild animal and any fast movement might spook him. "Thanks."

"And FYI, I wouldn't have shot you in the head."

I tried not to smile.

"What's so funny?"

"That is just one of the sweetest things anybody ever said to me."

He frowned.

"Kidding," I whispered.

Just the corner of his lip tipped up, a quick half-smile before he headed to the counter.

I sighed. If he didn't want me around, maybe it wasn't right for me to stay. After the Omaha job, I'd go back to the farm, but I would leave again—as soon as possible. And on my own terms.

Being with these guys showed me how huge the world was.

But when I tried to imagine what sort of life I might make, I couldn't think of one better than this—being with these lost Peter Pans with their road trips and the hotels. And the sex. And the connection, the sense of being on the edge of the whole world.

And being Isis.

Thor snoozed as soon as we were back on the road, splayed sideways, head on the door, legs on my lap.

I laid my hands on his legs, enjoying the solid feel of him. Our strange familiarity. His pant leg had bunched up just enough so that there was a gap between the cuff and the top of his sock, and I slid my hand to his calf, enjoying the pale, whispery-soft hairs that covered his skin there.

It was strange to feel this sense of domination over his sleeping body, though in truth, I felt a bit like small prey, enjoying the body of a sleeping lion. One who might wake up and consume me at any moment.

Which I certainly wouldn't mind.

I squeezed my thighs together, thinking about the things he'd said over lunch. The anticipation of more sex with my unpredictable, hot bandits, it was killing me a little.

But not as much as the suspense, the stuff he wouldn't say. *Some things that seem unpleasant in the telling can be quite enjoyable in the doing.*

What things?

The audiobook droned on. Outer space politics. I'd long ago stopped keeping the names and alien races straight. How could I concentrate on it when every sign and mile marker we passed put us closer to the next hotel and more kinky sex?

Also, now that Zeus had sort of apologized, would he join in? He seemed to be back in his cave up there, the sizzle of his gaze fixed firmly on the road. What did it mean? The anticipation was excruciating.

One time I looked over to find Thor awake, watching me, and I knew we were both thinking about the dirty things he'd said. A road trip had never made me feel quite so horny. Was it the vehicle's vibrations? The testosterone around me? Or Thor's talk?

Thor shifted his legs, rubbing against my pelvis, which I tilted up ever so slightly. His eyes darkened and he raised his brows. An invitation.

He came to me, kissed me.

"Twenty minutes," Odin said. We were turning off.

"Patience is a virtue," Thor said.

I closed my eyes as he kissed my neck. I was feeling anything but patient.

Not twenty minutes later, we were walking into a new fancy suite in a different fancy hotel—the grandly named *Imperium.* Our elite top-floor suite featured sweeping views, plus lots of marble and a hot tub, which looked very inviting to my cold toes.

Zeus studied the room service menu.

Thor gave me a heated look.

Odin took off his glasses, a move that never failed to thrill me.

He knew this, of course.

He stripped off his black shirt, then sat and yanked off his motorcycle boots.

"You guys have more costume changes than the Kardashians," I said.

"Did you just compare us to the Kardashians?" Odin asked. "Must we spank and fuck you before we even get into the hot tub?"

My stomach tightened. *Yes, please,* I thought. But then, my toes were still cold. Anyway, I could be spanked and fucked in the hot tub, right?

Isis liked to have her cake and eat it, too.

"Well, you said to always tell the truth of how I feel. So which look is real?"

Odin pushed down his pants, baring his sculpted body and half-hard cock. "All of them together are real. It's the whole gestalt." He went over and stuck a toe into the water. "Coming?"

"She doesn't want to get her hair mussed," Thor said to him, pulling off his own shirt.

"Is that so?" Odin stepped in, descended the steps, and sank into the water. "Even better. Come on, Isis."

I fingered the tie of my sundress bodice.

Zeus studied the menu fiercely, back on his policy of ignoring me.

Room service arrived with the cart of scotch and snacks they'd ordered at check-in.

This room service waiter, I'm happy to report, wasn't force-fed drugged champagne until he passed out. He simply parked the cart, took his tip, and turned to leave.

"Wait." Thor grabbed the vase of flowers from the cart and brought it to the waiter. "No flowers."

Yeah, buddy, or else Zeus will rip them up! I thought.

The waiter left. Thor bolted the door behind him, then he came back and played bartender.

Zeus picked up the phone to order. "Does anybody remember how the steaks are here? Anyone else eating?"

I grabbed a handful of Chex mix. "I'm good for now."

"Me too. I'll eat later. Sooner or later." Thor gazed at me, up and down. "Perhaps sooner *and* later. What do you think about that, Ice?"

I imagined his mouth on me. And Odin's hands. My libido went into throbbing overdrive. I wanted to say something witty, but all I could do was stand there trembling as he came up to me and undid the bow at the top of the bodice of my sundress.

Zeus proceeded to order enough food for a horse.

"So you guys aren't wary of room service now?" I asked.

Little crinkles appeared at the edges of Thor's blue eyes as he unlaced my dress little by little. "That won't be happening here." His confidence in this bordered on arrogance. "We don't get surprised twice in the same way." He unlaced another few inches.

I widened my eyes in the direction of Zeus. "Should we wait? You know..." I liked the idea of Zeus watching, but hated the idea of him not having the choice.

Thor raised his brows. "Is that a *no*?"

Zeus was on a different call now. He'd settled onto the couch across the room, talking with somebody at a repair shop or something—a conversation that sounded like it might go long.

Slowly, Thor pushed the straps over my shoulders.

My dress fell to the floor in a puddle around me.

"No," I whispered. "It's not a *no*, I mean..."

Thor smoothed his hands over my lacy underwear. "Zeus is a big boy." Wicked hands reached around to undo my bra. "He goes exactly where he pleases. Does what he pleases. We all do."

It made sense. Zeus wasn't the type to let himself be put out.

As soon as I was naked, Thor pointed to the tub. I strolled over, lowered myself in, and waded across to where Odin waited. I moved into his arms, into the mystery and thrill of not knowing what these two would do.

Thor got in and nestled onto the other side of me, sandwiching me.

Odin crept a hand over my thigh under the cover of the bubbly surface, reaching the desperately sensitive cleft between my legs.

One deft press of his fingers sent waves of pleasure through me.

Then Thor touched my belly, and I found their cocks.

It felt like a wonderful secret, their fingers on me under the water. Mine on them. Like we were in an erotic cocoon together.

Do anything you want to me, I wanted to say. *Anything you want*.

Zeus hung up the phone and stalked out of the room.

Thor stroked a finger through my tender folds. I could tell, just by the way his finger slid along, that I was slick, even under the water.

"Now," Odin said, hand creeping onto my belly, "whatever shall we do with you?" He kissed my cheek and my neck. My sex felt like heated honey. I drew teasing hands up both their legs. We were basically mauling each other in slow motion.

Suddenly Zeus was back again. He took off his boots, rolled up his jeans, grabbed the scotch bottle, and set it on the edge of the tub, right across from us. Then he sat down and swished his feet in the hot water, like it was all normal. Just another day in the tub with his pals.

I pressed my legs together, dislodging Thor's hand. Zeus probably couldn't see below the surface of the water, but still!

"What is happening here?" Thor intoned warningly.

I shot him a look.

Thor watched me with a mischievous expression. Not looking away, he said, "The water's fine, Zeus. You should get in." Then he slowly but firmly pulled my left leg toward him.

Excitement shot through my veins as Thor trailed a finger back up the inner line of my thigh.

Odin slid a hand over my shoulder and placed his other hand firmly on my right thigh, pulling it the other way, spreading my legs, giving Thor greater access.

I gasped softly and looked over at Zeus. I don't know if Zeus heard the gasp, but he glanced at me then, holding me with his beautiful eyes, lips pillowing into one another. A random dot of water from the spray had landed on his cheekbone and it glistened as brightly as the crystals on the chandelier above us.

He just sat there, all hungry disdain. What would it be like to see affection in his eyes?

Thor's very naughty fingers reached my yearning pussy. He slid one in, then out, then in. Then two fingers entered me, filling me. A thumb on my clit, rubbing slow and sure.

Lust pounded hot through my veins.

Warm breath tickled my cheek.

Could Zeus see how Thor was touching me? If Zeus didn't see, he had to know. It seemed excessive, what we were doing in front of him. Like eating pizza in front of a prisoner on a hunger strike.

My breath caught in my throat as Thor drew his fingers up through my hypersensitive folds. My belly quivered and still Zeus held my eyes. It was strangely hot, his watching, even with that dark edge.

Especially with that dark edge.

Thor pushed his fingers back into me, pressing, massaging my clit with his palm. I pressed my pelvis into his hand as the pleasure built. I was approaching the point of no return, right in front of Zeus. I could feel his stare on my skin, dark and hot.

Hold off, I told myself.

Odin dug his fingers into my thigh, spreading my legs wider for

Thor, who slid his fingers back into me, curling them just so. I exhaled softly, overcome with a rush of feeling.

Thor put his mouth to my ear. "Give it up."

He knew I was holding out.

We were locked into a strange game, the four of us.

Again, Thor put his mouth to my ear. "You know you want to," he whispered so that only I could hear. "And really, Isis, you have no choice. You know we will touch you and invade you and fuck you until you are completely given over."

"Is that so?" I asked coolly.

He got a playful look in his eyes. "We'll make it so," he said, moving his fingers in a new and exciting way, making the pleasure twist higher. Oh, it was good.

Again, I met Zeus's eyes. No way could he see anything but flesh-colored blobs under the surface.

Yet I'd never felt quite so exposed.

He was watching something more intimate than fingers on flesh; he was watching me get taken over, watching me lose the fight.

My breath shallowed in the grip of that gaze. My panting seemed to match the pulse of Thor's devilish fingers.

The room went hazy.

I felt Odin's teeth on my earlobe, a sting that had me close my eyes and almost lose it—*almost.*

I pulled myself back to Zeus's hard, covetous eyes once more.

I felt like I was falling into them. He knew the pleasure was building. He knew that I was losing. Was he trying to turn me on with that gaze? Or destroy me?

Maybe both.

"You know, yesterday was Ice's first time," Odin said, ever ready to embarrass me.

"Not my first time...*you* know." My face heated.

"First time with a trio," Odin said. "What did you think, Ice?"

Zeus swished his feet in the water, watching me.

I swallowed as Thor's fingers circled lazily around my clit. "You know what I thought," I said as casually as possible.

Thor slowed his clever fingers. "Give Zeus the report."

"Do I look like a porn magazine?" I said.

Odin said, "You looked like a porn magazine when you were masturbating in front of all of us yesterday. It was shameless."

"Wait, was that disobedience?" Thor stilled his fingers. "Refusing to give Zeus the report? Give Zeus the report on what you thought of what we did yesterday, or Odin will be wrathful."

I looked at Zeus across the pool, expecting more glowering, but instead I was hit with something else: loneliness. Zeus looked lonely.

"It was lovely," I said. "And very fun."

"That's not how I'd describe it," Odin said. "Isis, let me ask you, was it better than you imagined?"

Thor was toying with my nub again—he had me at the knife's edge of coming.

Breath heaved through my lungs.

"Was it better than you ever imagined?" Thor asked.

I was embarrassed and excited, being made to answer these questions while two men touched me in front of a third. "Yes, it was better."

"How was it better?" Odin pinched my nipple, rolling it.

My resistance was crumbling fast.

In my old life, my problem was taking too long. Now it was coming too fast, too early, or coming when commanded not to. It was like I'd landed in orgasm opposite world.

"Tell Zeus," Odin said.

I met his gaze. I wa tired of holding out. I wanted to give myself over—to give everything.

It was right then that I understood the biggest danger didn't come from their enemies or car chases or guns, but from our chemistry and our connection. I would rip myself apart for them.

"Tell Zeus," Odin commanded. "I won't ask you again."

I shook myself back to my senses and tried to sound breezy. "It just was more fun than it ever looked."

"Looked?" Odin said. "Online, you mean?"

My cheeks burned with heat. "Well," I said, "what else would I mean?"

Thor's fingers stopped. Odin loosened up.

"Oh, we need details on *this*," Odin said. "There's something you're hiding."

I swallowed, stunned, as usual, by his supernatural talent for zeroing in exactly where I didn't want him.

Zeus grabbed the bottle next to him and swigged some scotch.

Thor removed his hand, as if he wanted to allow me to concentrate.

"What do you like to watch?" Odin pursued.

I shrugged. "I don't know."

Chapter Fourteen

THOR SNUCK A HAND TO MY STOMACH AND TICKLED ME.

I yelped.

"Shh!" Odin scolded. "Do that again and we'll gag you. You'll tell us now. What are the things you watch? What do you have bookmarked?"

Thor tickled my stomach.

I squirmed and pushed off his hands. "Fuck off!"

Odin grabbed my arms and Thor tickled me some more and I was laughing like mad. "Stop!"

They stopped.

I grinned. "I won't tell. Ever!"

Thor was tickling me again and we were all laughing—even, much to my surprise, Zeus.

A knock at the door halted all of our fun. "Room service!"

Zeus was back to looking grim. "You kids want to take this into another room?"

"We most certainly will." Thor stood. "Isis, get out and go wait for us in the last bedroom. The one at the very end."

I hoisted myself out of the water with as much nonchalance as possible and wrapped myself up in a fluffy robe. "You won't get it out of me." I marched away. Had I really just said that? I felt half out of my mind.

"Come back here," Odin said.

I turned around. "What?"

Would they spank me right in front of Zeus? And what about the room service guy? Oh, God, would they spank me in front of the room service guy?

Odin pointed to the chair. "Leave the robe. You won't need it in there. And go lie on the bedspread and wait for us."

"On your *back*," Thor specified. "Eyes closed."

So outrageous. So bossy!

"*Oh-kay*." I pulled off the robe and set it on the chair, naked under the watchful eyes of all three of them now. I strolled into the back hallway, so casual, but really I was trembling with excitement.

I would give them anything.

It was weird to think that.

There were three bedrooms in the suite, maybe four. The place was a palace. I went into the last bedroom and lay on the bedspread, eyes closed, per my criminals' commands.

Well, I would give them *almost* anything, I decided. I wouldn't be giving them the truth about my cartoon porn habit. Let them try and get that out of me!

Though I wouldn't mind if they tried.

Or if they spanked me again.

Or really anything.

Water from my wet skin soaked the spread. It didn't matter; I felt like I was flying, completely out of control.

Shivers radiated over my skin.

Doors out there opened and closed, presumably for the room service guy.

My nipples felt cold and tight. I became aware of this buzz in my belly, erotic energy like buzzing static.

Male voices. The door again. That would be the room service

guy leaving. Zeus had his food. Thor and Odin would come in now.

I waited. Left to my own devices, I'd be lying on my side. It seemed more dignified. On my back felt less so.

This both appalled and excited me.

Footsteps! Heat and energy throbbed through me, and I watched the dark patterns on the insides of my lids, feeling impossibly wet and slick just from lying there.

Would Odin wear his glasses only to take them off? Because the way I was feeling, I might come just from that. Unless they made me *keep* my eyes closed. Then I wouldn't get to see him take his glasses off.

The footsteps went away. My blood raced.

Quiet.

Footsteps.

I clenched my eyes shut. I liked this sensory deprivation twist. My breath caught as I heard them come in. I felt something warm and soft draped over my eyes. "Lift your head."

Thor.

I complied and he tied something around my head, knotting it at the side.

A blindfold.

The bed depressed on one side of me. I felt the movement near my feet. Somebody crawling onto the bed. I heard the rip of Velcro and felt something soft around my right ankle, then my left.

Odin? Zeus?

"Hands behind your head, fingers laced," Thor said.

I did it, heart speeding as hands parted my thighs. I felt the pull of bonds at my ankles.

I gasped when something cold settled onto my belly—an ice cube! My tummy quivered. Let's just say an ice cube was the opposite of what I'd hoped for.

"Are you ready to talk?" Thor whispered into my ear.

"There's nothing to tell. So I watch porn. So what?"

Odin's voice came next. "There's more. You can't hold back."
So it was Odin down there, wielding the ice cube. Of course, because Zeus would be eating.

Also, the ice cube was Odin's style.

Odin traced a circle on my belly with the ice cube. I could handle it. It was just an ice cube.

The ice cube traveled down my belly and over the sensitive part of my pelvis.

Gasp! He would put it *there*?

"No," I whispered, not wanting my clit frozen.

But down it traveled. Slowly.

Excruciatingly slowly.

Water melted off it, dripping and drooling into the dips where my thighs began, cool rivulets over hot skin. Then I felt it hit my tender bud.

I sucked in a breath.

It was cold, but not as cold as I'd imagined. I felt the smooth form melting, drips rolling down my pussy.

The pressure felt good. Until it got cool. And cooler. I squirmed.

A hand clamped down on my thigh. "Details." Odin.

"What? Specific URLs?" I protested.

"Whatever you're hiding, that's what we want."

The ice was gone suddenly, replaced with a cool breeze. Odin blowing. I exhaled forcefully. It was so, so much sensation. Rough hands pushed my legs even farther apart.

A hot tongue traveled up the slick seam of my sex, up, up to the tender nub, ending with a firm, hard lick. I gasped as he licked again. Again.

I was warming, coming to life. The warmth and rubbing of Odin's tongue felt better than anything I could imagine. "Yes," I moaned.

I felt a mouth on my breast now, sucking, laving my nipple. It was heaven. I moaned and squirmed, about to go over the edge. This was no punishment at all. It was nirvana.

Until they stopped.

"No," I panted.

"Details." Odin. "What is it that you won't tell? A humiliation thing? Vacuums? Ropes? A kind of binding?"

"No, not like that."

"Clamps?" Thor asked. "Because we can do that."

I shook my head, heart pounding. "I know nothing of clamps!" Possibly a too-jokey answer, because I felt a cold drip on my stomach. "No!" I hissed. But yes, it was that again, the ice cube, now held firmly to my belly button.

"God!" My belly quivered.

"It must be very *fucking-g* dirty," Odin said. "Oh, I do want to hear."

I shook my head.

"Have it your way."

The ice cube traveled down over the tender, sensitive skin of my pelvis and over my mound to my slick seam. I tried in vain to draw my legs together, fighting against the ankle bonds.

I felt the ice cube there, then the hot tongue was back.

I moved along with it.

Heat bloomed through me.

Then it stopped.

"Come back!" I gasped.

Nothing.

"I'll tell!"

"We're waiting."

"Cartoons."

"What?" Surprised amusement played in Thor's voice.

"More details," Odin said.

"Please," I said.

"Tell us."

"Half-elf girls being ravished, okay? Or girls with tails. You know, cartoon porn."

"You're shitting us," Odin said.

"I'm not!" I protested.

Thor snickered.

"It's not funny," I said. "It's hot."

"Ravished how?"

"Just ravished."

Now there was the cool air. The cool air treatment again, which was both worse and better.

I writhed and gasped. I just wanted the tongue back!

"How?" Thor demanded.

Odin's tongue was back. I thought I would go mad from the sensation of him drawing it up to my outrageously sensitized clit.

"By woodland guys," I panted. "I'll tell you everything, everything, just don't stop again. Don't do the ice thing again."

"Describe them and tell us what they do to her," Thor commanded. "But if you stop talking, the ice comes back, and it stays until it melts."

Odin licked me as I breathlessly described everything about the stuff I'd watched, how they always tied the girl up and fucked her. He stopped when I so much as paused in my breathless recounting, so I kept on, trying to think of any details. I liked when they fingered her asshole, or forced her legs apart and fucked her, or two of them fucked her at once, like she's riding one while the other fucks her ass.

They wanted more, so I kept on.

The dudes usually wore caps, often Robin Hood-type outfits—tights and scabbards. The girl had to be kind of a captive, but into it. I didn't like when the girl cried. I would turn those ones right off. The girl could struggle, but I had to know she was into it. I liked when they locked her into old-fash-

ioned-looking stocks, forcing her into helplessly obscene posi-
tions to be fucked.

"No spanking?"

"I never saw the upside in that," I blurted as Odin's warm,
talented tongue flattened in a luscious way. "I might now."

I felt two fingers slide into my slick hole and curl just so.

"Oh, God, please," I gasped,

The fingers moved strongly in me, moving in me in a rhythm,
in and out and in and out, as his tongue mirrored the motion.

"More," Thor said. "Say more."

"There is no more. They usually find her wandering in the
woods..." I began to rock my hips, feeling like I was being sucked
into a black hole of pure pleasure, which, let's face it, I was.

"Do you want him to stop?" Thor asked.

Odin stopped.

"Wandering around gathering flowers!" I blurted, and he
started up again. "Daisies. Friend to woodland creatures. Squirrels
sometimes watch them take her, chattering and chewing on nuts
while they take her brutishly..."

I was partly making stuff up now. I would've said anything to
keep him going, licking me right over the edge, and oh, it was
exquisite all the way down—down and down and down.

Suddenly, my mind and body exploded into an abyss of an
orgasm. Wave after wave pulsated through me, washing me with
sensation, from the top of my head to my toes.

I heard myself bleat out a strangled kind of cry, very woodland-
animal-esque.

Thor murmured something to Odin, but I couldn't make out
a word of it, what with the sparkles that were holding a rave inside
my body, complete with glow-sticks and pulsating music.

I came down eventually, feeling like a floppy thing washed up
on a beach.

Silence.

"Two woodland guys?" Thor finally said. "Odin, we're gonna have to buy some little green hats."

I tore off my blindfold and hit Thor with it.

He grabbed my wrists and pinned me to the bed. "That was so freaking hot."

"It *was* hot." Odin released my ankles from their bonds and crawled onto the bed on the other side of me, heavy hand on my belly, cock nudging at my hip. "Did you think that was hot, Zeus?" Odin asked.

I jerked my head up to see Zeus, standing at the doorway, arms folded over his chest.

Shit!

He'd been watching?

Chapter Fifteen

"So that's what girls like? Porn cartoons?" Zeus said. "I was always wondering who the fuck watches those."

With that, he left.

"We need to get some sort of rustic stocks," Odin said. "We never thought of that for our hideout."

Thor grinned. "And bows and arrows."

"He was watching the whole time? And I didn't know?" I asked.

"Do you have a problem with that?" Odin said. His five-o'clock shadow was more a ten o'clock shadow now, adding to his smoldering, glittering heat. He had a tiny scar at the top of his cheekbone, I noticed, that the glasses hid.

"I like to know." So he'd been watching. The idea of somebody watching made it more exciting...but the idea of Zeus watching was next level.

"Ears, we'll get you ears," Thor said, releasing my arms, trailing a finger along my ear. He kissed me there.

"Is that what he does?" I asked. "Watch?"

"He was a participant," Odin said. "In the old days."

Thor whispered, "At least he came in. It's good. It's a start."

"You guys have a hideout?" I asked.

"Several." Odin caressed my belly. Thor had his fingers on my nipple. I reached aside and touched his taut arm, his shoulder. I reached down and found Thor's cock, then Odin's. We fell into a rhythm. Soon I was overwhelmed by the sensation of many hands and tongues on me, and access to multiple cocks.

In this, too, it was a lot like the ski jump—overwhelming and confusing until you released yourself to it, and then it was the best thing in the world.

"I want you to take me, to fill me," I whispered. "Just fuck me!"

"We're getting to it."

I wrapped my fingers around Thor's silky, steely hardness. Odin's had gone out of reach, but I grabbed his hair and pulled him into me. He kissed me, and then he bit my lip, and by the way he was breathing, I knew he was doing himself. Which was so hot.

"You want Zeus to join?" Odin breathed.

"Now?"

"He won't now, but at some point?"

"Well, yes," I said. I felt surprised that wasn't obvious. "It's not something I've ever done, you know..." Thor was so hard in my hand. It was difficult to concentrate. I was sick of concentrating.

"Three woodsmen?" Thor asked. "You don't know how to do three woodsmen? If only there were some diagrams or drawings we could access. If only it was animated so that you could see—"

"Don't make fun," I said.

"Don't worry about the logistics, Isis," Odin said. "We can make any kind of fucking work. We're experts, baby."

I smiled, feeling intoxicated, greedy. I wanted to fuck, to be filled. "Good," I said, tired of words. Then, "More."

Odin cupped my mound.

"God, yes," I breathed.

"Turn over," Odin whispered gruffly.

I released Thor and turned onto my belly, quivering with anticipation.

"No," Odin said, caressing my ass. "On your knees."

I got on my knees there on the bed. My pussy felt extra slick now, exposed to the cool air. Would they spank me? I wasn't aware of having done anything wrong, but I had definitely talked back once or twice.

Odin slid up to sit back against the headboard, gazing hard into my eyes. "I want you to suck me like you did Thor. And you remember how that goes? Do it in a way that makes you available to Thor. Spread your legs, baby."

I complied.

"Thor, get back there and fuck her. Not in the ass. And she needs you to touch her to get her off. But I say when she comes."

So many commands! And he knew I needed to be touched to get off. Odin was like the Sherlock Holmes of sex.

I bent to Odin and took just the head of his cock in my mouth, thinking to do some fancy tongue thing. I was so horny again.

Crinkling behind me. A condom.

"No, no, no." Odin grabbed my hair and forced my head down onto him, clearly in the mood to fuck my mouth. "Hard," he said. "I've been waiting. Hard, hard. And grab it with your hand."

More commands. A dark thrill speared through me as I grabbed him at the base with one hand and sucked him like he wanted.

And then I felt the probe of Thor's cock at my clit, sliding up and down, spreading juices all around. All the nerves back there felt exposed and tingly, and I felt desperate to have him inside me.

"My balls," Odin said, guiding my hand down to cup them.

Thor nudged at my entrance with the blunt, fat tip of his cock.

I shivered right to the top of my head, feeling like I might come already.

"You are so freaking wet," Thor said, pressing just the head of his cock into my slick channel. "Oh," he panted, filling me further.

I stopped to enjoy the sensation of him penetrating me deeply, brutally.

Odin growled and took control of my hair again, pushing lightly on my head, reminding me of my responsibility to his own cock as Thor withdrew and plunged into me, taking me. He fucked me, and I sucked Odin, using my hand to stroke his fabulously thick root. Then Thor reached around and rubbed my clit. It was like the three of us were all connected, fucking each other, panting along with each other, waves of erotic energy rolling between us.

No, it was *more*.

It was like we created a single animal—one lusty, pleasure-seeking being. I'd never felt anything like it in my life, this heat and energy, and the way the three of us together tripled it.

"A little teeth," Odin grated.

I let my teeth graze up and down his shaft.

He hissed out a breath and set a new rhythm with his hand, forcing my head and tweaking my nipple with his free hand.

I could tell he was on the edge. I wanted to push him over, concentrate only on him. But the combo of us was too wonderful to isolate one thing. Thor fucked me harder, rubbing me with a smooth, slick finger, long strokes up and down. His finger felt strangely long.

Odin gripped my hair tightly, a naughty new note for our erotic symphony.

Somebody panted. Waves built in me. I was about to come. I'd need to think of something horrible if I wanted to not come.

Thankfully Odin put me out of my misery. "Let go, Isis, let it take you," he said. "Come for us."

I was so there. His words tipped me right over the edge into a chaos of sensation.

Waves pounded through my sex, my belly, my eyes.

Odin clamped his hand harder on my head for one final push. His cock vibrated in my mouth, spewing cum into my throat.

"Fuck, mother of fuck," Thor said as he drove into me, grip tightening on my hips, ferociously invading me. "Fuck!"

Odin's cock was motionless in my mouth, but his hand had changed; instead of the commanding head-pushing, he was stroking my hair. "Isis," he whispered as I pulled my mouth off him.

I kissed his brown-bronze stomach and nuzzled the line of hair up from his belly button, partly to wipe my lips, and partly because I just wanted to. I kissed up and up. Thor pulled out of me, and Odin got up on his knees and kissed me—passionately.

Romantically.

We'd done so much fucking and mindfucking that this romantic kiss came as a shock, and it took my breath away. I kissed him back, enjoying him, feeling him.

I was aware of Thor getting off the bed, the bathroom light flipping on, and still Odin kissed me. Then he lowered me onto my back and crouched over me on all fours, hands planted on the sides of my shoulders, knees on the sides of my knees, and he loomed over me, and we just looked into each other's eyes.

I liked it—*loved it*—lying naked underneath this man I barely knew, yet my sense of connection to him was beyond what I had with most people in my life. And I suppose we'd been through so much intensity together, he and I. And Thor and Zeus.

"I felt like we were one thing," I said. "The three of us."

Pain in Odin's eyes. "I know," he said. He lowered himself and stretched out next to me, lying half on top of me, draping an arm possessively on my stomach.

Was he sad that I'd be leaving?

Thor came back in and lay behind Odin, draping an arm around the both of us.

It surprised me, yet didn't, that they'd feel so comfortable touching each other like that. Not sexual, but just comfortable. I wanted more.

"Zeus won't let you stay," Odin said, as if reading my mind.

Thor set his chin on Odin's arm.

Odin turned his head and glanced up at Thor. Something passed between the two men, I didn't know what.

So my bank robbers would eject me, I thought with a pang of sadness.

But I wouldn't stay in Baylortown—I knew now that I couldn't. That would be their gift to me.

Maybe I could use my share of the loot to start an adventure outfit of some kind after college. My bungee jumping school plan. It didn't feel as exciting as it used to. Bungee jumping seemed boring and sad compared to being with my bank robbers.

Chapter Sixteen

I woke up the next morning alone in the bed. I had dim memories of Thor having spent the night there with me, Odin maybe part of it.

I got into the shower and let the hot water pound on my skin, thinking about my sisters. What was going on? Surely they'd know from my Paris Hilton message that I was okay.

I put on my bathrobe, wondering if Thor and Odin would want to have sex right away. Our bargain was that I'd say yes, like I belonged to them.

It was all very wrong in a way that I loved.

I slipped out the door. Masculine murmurs and the aroma of coffee came from the direction of the main room. The murmurs sounded more and more like arguing as I neared. Something about somebody being unreasonable.

The talking stopped when I arrived.

"Good morning, comrades," I said.

Zeus's motorcycle-boot-clad feet were up on the table. He looked like like a dangerous mercenary on mercenary casual day in his dark jeans and green military-issue sweater.

Thor wore a similar outfit, but he'd added a baseball cap.

Odin was hunched over the coffee table rubbing a black piece of metal with a cloth.

"She walks, she talks," he said.

Hardware-looking things were strewn out in front of him. It took me a while of staring to get that those were gun parts.

Lots of them.

I averted my eyes from all the dangerous and probably illegal firepower.

But, *hello*, it wasn't anything I hadn't seen before...*while they were robbing a bank and taking me hostage.*

Thor shoved a chair out with his foot. "Saved you a seat."

It touched me that they'd set a place for me.

Enjoy it while you can, I thought.

"You and your sheep farm and your sisters are all over TV," Zeus grumbled.

"Really? Like what? How do they seem?"

"We should've dumped you if we'd known what was good for us," he said, ignoring my questions.

"I'm glad you didn't," I said, voice small.

Zeus scowled.

But they were good for their promises, these guys. Maybe they had a messed-up code by some standard—okay, most standards—but hey, they had a code.

Zeus eyed me as I sat. "Get the laptop, Thor."

"Let her have some coffee first," Thor said. "Cream?"

"Oh, yes, please. And sugar, thanks."

Thor smiled wickedly, pushing the little china vessels across the table to me. "Cream and sugar it is, then."

Leave it to Thor to make even that exchange sound dirty. I fixed up my coffee and sipped, coming to life as the caffeine infused my brain.

Thor pulled a laptop out of a black case and set it up on the table in front of me. "You can't freak out," he said.

"I won't," I said.

Thor clicked to a northern Wisconsin news station. I could feel Zeus watching me as a clip started to play. A news conference started with the Baylortown police answering questions. The time stamp was 8 p.m. last night, central time. So after I'd ordered the quilt. Around the time I was cavorting in a hot tub with my two bandits.

Some police chief I'd never heard of was heading the investigation. They *had no leads at this time*.

"Because we're *fucking-g awesome*," Odin said from the couch.

They were *pursuing several avenues that could yield promise*. No, they couldn't comment further.

"Code for not a *fucking-g* clue," Odin added. "Nobody catches us."

And then my three sisters filed up to the microphone, bright red hair, pale skin. Candy, who'd just graduated high school, and my youngest sister, fifteen-year-old Kaitlin, were crying.

My heart lurched.

"Bring Melinda home, she's done nothing to you!" Kaitlin sobbed.

Vanessa, the oldest of my younger sisters, took the microphone then. "We ask that you bring Melinda back to us. We lost our parents and she's all we have. All the money in the world can't make up for our sister." She changed her demeanor, stared into the camera. "Melinda, we're not going to give up on you. You've done everything for us. We're going to get you home. We'll make everything right. We need you and miss you."

Candy took the microphone. "Bring our sister home, please."

I pressed my hand to my mouth, willing myself not to cry. Had they not gotten the Paris Hilton message? Did they not understand that I was okay? I wished I could reassure them. Did they not see that part of the message about the happy home?

Then there were questions for some other official. Zeus shut the laptop. "The rest is bullshit. What do you say?"

I took a deep breath. "Shit."

Zeus said, "You can go back, you know. It's been two days. This is plausible."

"I'm aware of that."

Zeus crossed his arms. "Anything pop out?"

"Like what?"

"You know your sisters. You see something we didn't?"

"I can't tell if they understood the message. You know, with the quilt order. The orders feed into email and Vanessa would've checked. Candy and Kaitlin seemed so upset, though. But assuming Vanessa got the message and understood, she wouldn't have told Candy or Kaitlin." I pondered. "Vanessa said that one thing— 'All the money in the world can't make up for our sister.' I think she's sorry I had to take the bank job. And she knows I slid them that Paris Hilton comforter order."

"It's pretty clear they need you home," Zeus said.

"They *need* me, yes," I said. "But they don't need me home. Right now, they're better off with me here. I think we've established that."

"The fuck we've established that," Zeus said. "I don't see it."

Thor shot him a look. "You gonna stop riding her on this anytime soon?"

Zeus grunted.

"Say what you want," I said to Zeus. "Those three, they love the farm. They need me to help support it, and yeah, we're sisters, we love each other. But I've only ever wanted to leave. They love it there." For the first time, I felt a little resentful about it.

Why did I have to stay all those years? Why did I have to feel guilty for a couple days of freedom?

It was irrational to be angry with them, I knew that, but still.

"What?" Thor came behind me and massaged my shoulders.

"What is it?"

"It's just that, when my folks died, I didn't just lose the two most important people in my life. It put an end to all my dreams. I was the only adult and I *had* to stay, you know? I had to keep things going. For six years I put everything on hold. But the three of them are adults now. And they have twenty grand. There're people they can hire." I stared straight at Zeus. "You don't want me along with you, Zeus, and I get that. But after everything that's happened? I need to be free. When our gig is up, fine, I'll do what's best for the group. I'll go back to Baylortown and do whatever you need me to do to make this look good. You know I can pull it off. But after that, I'm off. I'll find a way to get them money, but it's not going to be stitching quilts or feeding sheep or working as a teller in a pervert's bank."

"Alrighty, then," Zeus said.

"And don't tell me whether they need me or not, or how they need me. I get that they miss me, but I'm doing some good for the farm right now, and I'll be home soon enough. We're getting publicity and we can't be foreclosed. I don't see why I can't enjoy that, and why you have to make me the bad guy."

Snicks and clacks from the couch. Odin shoved a clip into a gun and stood up. Like Zeus, he was dressed in mercenary casual. He strolled over and pointed a giant gun at an ugly painting of a cabin with a candle in the window. "Pow!" Odin said.

"It's inappropriate to shoot the bad art," I said.

Odin squinted. "We're criminals, baby. Everything we do is inappropriate."

I grinned. If I were writing an adventure essay about this experience, I would definitely use that line. But of course, I wouldn't be writing this up.

Zeus wandered over to the coffee table and picked out a gun, then he went and stood by Odin and aimed at the picture. "Daddy wants to go to the range."

"Let's hit it before we sit on the bank." Odin was still aiming, squinting. Maybe he was checking the sights or something. They made quite the picture. Still life with outlaws.

Zeus shoved his gun into a holster under his sweater. "You two stay here. Got it? Stay out of trouble."

"Don't worry," Thor said.

Zeus and Odin left soon after.

I poured more coffee. "No shooting range for you?"

Thor stared into his coffee. "I'm not much for it."

"But you carry a gun," I observed.

"We *are* criminals." The bitter edge in Thor's voice told me he didn't find the term as amusing as Odin did. It struck me that *criminals* was a name that was *applied* to them, not one they'd chosen.

At the bank, we tellers had once heard Hank Vernon call us *ignorant bitches* and thereafter, we'd use it on one another, like, *come on, share your cookies with the rest of us ignorant bitches.* Using the phrase on ourselves gave us power. Showed we were more. With a little bit of anger and hate in the mix.

That's the way Thor used the word criminal. It made me wonder who he hated.

"Did you ever have to shoot at a person?" I asked.

He crumbled a scone, looking thoughtful, one chunk of hair over his eyes. "Once," he said, softly. It weighed on him—grief, guilt—I couldn't tell how it weighed, only *that* it weighed. I got up and went behind where he sat, put my hands on his shoulders and rubbed gently.

Thor sighed when I touched him like that. The sigh sounded like relief, like he needed empathy. Thor was a doctor, and he clearly loved people, yet he'd shot and maybe killed a person. I stayed there, consoling him, wanting to rub the hurt away, knowing I couldn't.

He pushed away his plate. "Get dressed, we have errands to run."

"But Zeus and Odin took the van."

He looked up with a devilish smile. "You think we need the van to run an errand? Put on that sundress again."

I narrowed my eyes. Odin and Zeus had told us to stay put. What errands did Thor suddenly want to run? I went to put on my sundress. When I came out, he was nowhere. I poured another cup of coffee and went online to www.SunnySistersSheepFarm.com.

There was the home page with its photo of the four of us girls holding hands surrounded by sheep. I'd worked hard on that site; building it turned out to be 80% tutorial watching and 20% not finding the answer in a tutorial.

There was a page where I described the artisan blue cheese we make. Small-batch cheese making is a long, multi-staged process; one of my sisters would be taking over my parts. Probably Vanessa. When I went to the page for the natural wool comforters we make, I saw that Vanessa had raised the price of our double from $280 to $420, and that they were delivering in seven to ten weeks, whereas it used to be three to five.

Were they getting a ton of orders? That had to be why!

I clicked to the blog and saw a new entry, dated this morning, entitled "Update on our sister," with a photo of me with my formerly long red hair.

Thank you to everyone for the outpouring of support, prayers, and well wishes. Thanks to the kindness of people, so many that we do not even know, our sister will have a farm to come back to. Please continue to pray and to keep an eye out for her.

We are also grateful for the comforter orders pouring in, but of course, most of all, we need our sister.

Melinda, if you're reading this, we miss you so much! We love you. We know, also, how hard you worked and how much we were suffocating you. When you come back, we'll make it up to you, and this will include tater tots with every meal, Candy doing the dishes, a way to send you around the world to make connections with retail outlets, and of course, no more working at a bank ever again! We will give you the Paris Hilton treatment! Please, bank robbers, let our sister come home!

I knew how Vanessa's mind worked—the fact that she'd mentioned Paris Hilton was significant. It was like a secret code, telling me she'd for sure gotten my message, and understood that I was happy being away. She wouldn't have apologized like that otherwise.

I wished I could leave a comment on the post. *It's not about you!* I would say. *Don't feel guilty! Be happy for me and let me do this!*

Way too risky.

We suffocated you…

I scrolled to the older entries, but it was all my writing, posts about different sheep in the dairy flock and shearing and all that. Our Friesago was up for an award.

Maybe the judges would give us a pity trophy.

Twenty minutes later, Thor and I were slipping out the back of the hotel. We strolled through the pool area and out to the far section of the parking lot.

Thor stopped in front of a silver Camaro. "Hello, lover." He pulled a long, flat piece of metal from his sports coat and shoved it roughly against the window and down into the door housing.

I gasped. "What are you doing?"

"Opening the door."

"What the hell?"

"Relax."

"I thought you were the doctor," I said.

"The doctor with skills." He jerked out the strip and pulled open the door. The horn began to honk, and he dove under the dash and did something I couldn't see to stop it. A minute later, the car roared to life. He got out and smiled at me, all mischievous and gorgeous.

"I can't believe you just did that."

He leaned back on the car and motioned for me to get in the driver's seat. "You're driving."

"A stolen car?"

"You can drive stick, can't you?"

"Hello, it's *stolen*." Playfully, I grabbed the front of his shirt and jerked it back and forth.

He put his hands on my hips and pulled me to him. "And? You want to be the driver on a job, and you can't drive a stolen car?"

"It's not an issue of *can*. I can drive it." I leaned fully into him, pressing him against the car, letting him take my weight, enjoying the feel of his cock at my pelvis.

He kissed my neck. "Driving in a crime situation is different from driving in a normal situation. We're going across town to get some catfish sandwiches for the guys for lunch. Let's see if you have the nerve."

"Did you just think of this? Is this something Odin and Zeus are on board with?"

"You want to stand here arguing until the owner comes back? Can you drive it or not?"

"Of course I can." I was proud of being a girl who was good at driving stick. I swung in.

"Out," he said.

Aha, so he was just seeing if I *would*, I thought. I got out of the car again.

He lowered his voice. "Remove your panties."

Chapter Seventeen

"Excuse me?" Thor wanted me to remove my panties, now?

"Don't argue."

My blood raced. I had this dim thought that maybe it was a test. That other girl, Venus, had driven for them. "You'll see I can drive under any and all conditions."

Confidently, I took off my panties, handed them over, and got in.

He stuffed them in his pocket and got in the passenger side.

I put it into gear and slammed out of there.

"Right here and your first left." His instructions took me across a pretty crowded few lanes and then left. "Left again. You drive a Camaro before?"

"No."

He looked at me suspiciously.

"I'm from a farm, dude," I said. "You start young on a farm, and you handle a lot of different vehicles in a lot of different circumstances. With sheep running all around."

He pointed left. Taking me back across two lanes. So...circles.

"You think I might be able to stay," I said. "You think there's a chance. Or you wouldn't want to see me drive. Right?"

"Nothing's changed, but we need you to sit with the car tomorrow."

"I'd be a great driver. And I know how banks work, don't I? I am a total asset. Not to mention a fellow god." I smiled calmly at him but really, driving a stolen car freaked me out. I wished we were back at the hotel having sex.

"You wouldn't actually drive for the getaway. You would just keep the car running for us. Running and available to blast out. And call us if there's any heat, and you'd move it if it got blocked. For the getaway part, you'd move over as soon as we came out and Zeus would drive."

He reached over and tugged at the string holding my dress bodice, loosening the tie.

I laughed. "What are you doing?"

"Keep driving." His fingertips brushed my nipples, which were instantly hard.

"I'm trying to drive in traffic!" I slapped away his hands, stunned at his recklessness.

"You'd better concentrate, then." He unlaced my bodice some more, so that my boobs were almost hanging out. It was kind of a rush because I was driving a stolen car and trying to drive well; in this way, I was as immobilized as if I were tied up.

"You are seriously unhinged." At a stoplight, I tightened my dress top back up and made a double bow. "God!" Then the light turned green.

"Left lane," he said.

I put on the blinker and changed lanes. Suddenly his fingers were on my bodice, loosening the ties again. "You are to leave them like this. This is part of the test."

I laughed. "Have you lost your mind?"

"A little," he said. My pulse raced as he pushed his hand into my dress front and fingered my nipple. I gasped when he squeezed it—my nipple was a rock-hard bundle of screaming nerves, and the excitement shot clear through me. When he finally took back his exquisitely teasing fingers, the edges of my bodice continued to rub my nipples, driving me a little bit wild.

He directed me around town. Was he looking for something? The catfish place?

We hit a four-lane road with lots of lights and traffic. I felt I was doing pretty well, considering the distractions.

He put his hand on my thigh and slid it up under my dress.

"Oh my god!" I pushed his hand away and downshifted. "Do you want to get us into an accident?"

"Is that a Mississippi?"

"No," I whispered.

His hand was back on my thigh. "Push me away again and you'll get more than a spanking. Don't think we can't escalate."

"Excuse me, I'm trying to drive a stolen car!"

"You can multitask, can't you, Ice? Think of this as a skills test."

Up, up, up went his fingers pressing lengthwise into my cleft. He drew them up, then down, then up in long, slow strokes of his, like a violin player might stroke a violin with a bow.

Warmth washed over me.

I pushed my pelvis into his hand at a stoplight, craving more pressure.

"You are so wet." He withdrew his fingers and pressed them into his mouth. "I want to fuck you every way to Sunday right now."

"We could pull over," I offered.

He pushed up my dress so that my pussy was totally exposed. "You want me to fuck you in a stolen car?"

"Yes," I breathed. And I wanted the fingers back.

He obliged as the light turned green.

"Ungh," I said as he thrust two fingers in, rubbing me with his thumb all the while. "We should park."

"I think I like you like this. Strapped in. Driving. A little bit helpless."

I swallowed, shifted. I *was* helpless—in a way I'd never been before. It was as if my body were his, completely separated from my mind, from the attention I needed for the road. This was a dangerous game.

And it thrilled me to pieces.

I gyrated a little.

"And you will stay like this until I'm finished with you," he said.

"What if I crash us?"

"Don't."

"What would Odin and Zeus say about this?"

"Oz isn't in the car with us." He continued stroking me with wicked fingers.

"Oz?"

"Oz. Odin and Zeus."

I exhaled sharply as he rubbed in a new way, curling those fingers inside me, creating the best sensation ever. I really wanted to pull over and freely throb with pleasure.

"I don't think Oz would approve," I said, fighting to concentrate on the road.

"Agreed."

Criminals, I thought dimly, *are more outrageous than other people.*

"Look, look, look—" He pointed ahead. "There's a cop up there."

"Crap!" My libido party halted.

His fingers didn't.

"Drive natural. Go the speed limit." He kept touching me—lewdly, expertly. "I could make you come at any time."

I pushed away his hand.

"Uh-uh-uh. Don't do that." He put it back. "And if you got arrested right now," Thor said, rubbing my clit, "driving this with me, they'd think it was an inside job. The job at your bank. You'd be thrown in jail."

He was playing a reckless game. Should I say Mississippi? "I would never want to play chicken with you."

"Is that a Mississippi?" he asked.

"Hell no." I kept my attention on the road.

Thor grinned.

It came to me then that Thor was like the overdue-for-an-inspection wooden roller coaster at a small county fair—thrilling and quite possibly dangerous.

Odin was more like the sleek and twisting metal roller coaster at the mammoth theme park, scientifically designed for maximum thrills.

Zeus was the cave of mystery, like you know it's dangerous in there but you still want in.

Odin and Zeus would definitely not think this joyride of ours was okay, but there was no way I'd say *Mississippi.*

"What are you thinking about?"

"What kind of amusement park rides you guys would be."

He narrowed his eyes at me. "Go the speed limit, even if you have to pass him." He put in two fingers. It was all so freaky hot, but I was starting to handle it—my mind on driving, on the cop, while Thor stroked my sex, my body hovering on the verge of total nuclear orgasm.

I concentrated on the road, panting. "What would you be doing if I hadn't shown up? Setting fires in the hotel room?"

He smiled. "Cut in front of him now."

"Let me get some distance."

"Now," Thor said.

"Are you shitting me?"

"You'll do it if you want to be our driver. I need to see you'll listen."

"This isn't a sex game."

"It's more important," he snapped. "Fuck, you're tight. Have I told you that?" And then he withdrew his fingers from me, rubbing me lazily with the back of his thumb.

I maneuvered in front of the cop. "Jesus," I said, watching the rearview mirror.

Thor, I noticed, was watching it a lot, too.

I was starting to relax. I could do this. "If that cop was going to do something, he would've done it by now."

"Maybe," Thor said, pushing a finger back down, down between my butt cheeks, which were compressed on the seat.

"You wouldn't," I gulped.

"Shut up and drive," he commanded, pressing a wet finger over the pucker of my ass. I gasped as he pressed a little way into me, filling me with a pleasurable sensation that spread clear up to my head.

"You might have to take the wheel," I whispered deliriously.

"You're doing great, baby. Keep your hands at the ten o'clock and two o'clock position."

His finger was probably only buried in my asshole as far as a knuckle, but it felt like a lot more, especially when he moved it around. His thumb sped up on my clit. It was amazing what he could do with one hand. I watched the cop in the rearview mirror as the pleasure built. It was all I could do not to pass out from pure adrenaline.

Finally a red light. I stopped, tipped my head back on the headrest, and looked over at him.

"Look at you," he said. "I love looking at you when you're a little gone like this."

I loved looking at him, too. And I loved being gone. I wanted to kiss him.

He stroked my cleft with a knuckle now, up and down and up and down, still with that finger stuck in my ass. It was heaven and hell all mixed together, having to stay gripping the wheel for this. I closed my eyes in the face of the mounting sensation.

"Green."

"What?" I asked.

"Green! Go!"

I pulled my mind back together, released the clutch, and shifted. "You are so evil."

"And you aren't?"

As I drove on, he moved his finger, which was still gripped by my asshole—he wasn't putting it in any farther, but the way he was moving it was making me crazy. It was the most thrilling thing ever!

"Aren't you?"

"Yes," I said, not remembering what the question was.

He pushed in a little now, probing at me, and at the same time, stroked my clit harder with his slicked thumb. Then he leaned over, putting his mouth near my ear. "Come for me."

Eep!

"Come for me," he commanded in his rumbly way. Then he tweaked my asshole, and I was gone, rocked with a mind-bending climax. I kept my eyes on the road and my mind on driving as the waves of pleasure surged through me.

"Uhhh," I breathed, lost.

He grabbed the wheel at one point. Had that been his backup all along? To grab the wheel? "Keep it together," he said, laughing.

He let up when we hit another red light.

I looked over at him, unsure whether I should kiss him or punch him in the face.

He leaned back and set his head against the headrest. "That was fun."

More than fun. It was a complete rush.

I felt...exhilarated.

"We need to get some lube, though. I cannot wait to bury my cock in that deadly tight ass of yours. Turn right at the next light. Has anybody ever fucked that awesome little asshole of yours?"

"Excuse?"

"Green."

"Crap." I started back up and took the next right. Getting away from the cop was such a relief. "I can't believe we just did that."

Thor laughed. "Are you avoiding my question?"

"No," I said. "No, never."

"You'll like it. We'll make it good, Isis. Though it is best to work up to it. In fact, it really is best to work up to it over a few days' time. For somebody who's never done it. So tight like you."

There was this silence in the car after that. Because we didn't have *time* to work up to it.

I sighed. "I'm a sad panda that we don't have time to work up to buttfucking."

He shifted his eyes my way. He was a sad panda, too. More of a sad puma. A slightly dangerous yet sad puma.

"I wish you could've seen our hideout. Especially our California one. Some of the shit we have there...let's just say we have a dedicated room."

"Dedicated to what?"

"To fucking. And punishing naughty goddesses who don't do as they're told."

My belly went floaty. The room sounded exciting and dangerous and horrible and wonderful. And I would never get to see it.

"On the bright side, you seem perfectly capable of driving the car under intense pressure and distraction."

I hit his shoulder. He caught my wrist, kissed my hand.

"You are a freak," I said.

He kissed a finger.

It was then I thought about what he'd said about Venus subconsciously wanting to get caught. "Are you going to tell Odin and Zeus about this afternoon drive of ours?"

"Maybe. If I feel like it," he said.

I took my hand from him. "It was kind of risky. Convince me why it was different than Venus subconsciously wanting to get caught."

"How it was *different?*" He sounded offended, and when I looked over, his eyes had lost their friendly twinkle. "Do *you* want us to get caught?" he demanded.

"Of course not," I said.

"Funny, you're the one who wouldn't say *Mississippi*. You had a chance to say Mississippi and put a stop to it, and you chose not to. Why was that?"

I was sort of stunned by this. He had a point. We'd both been playing the game.

"Why?"

"I wanted to keep going," I confessed. "I wanted to keep pushing it."

"And?"

"It was fun and exciting."

He put his feet up on the dashboard. "One of the perks of being an outlaw is that you get to *act* like a motherfucking outlaw.

I kind of loved that. These were my people, I realized. "You think Zeus could ever change his mind?"

"His thing with Venus, it runs deep," Thor said. "I don't see him changing his mind too easily."

"You need a driver. Or at least a car sitter, whatever. You didn't have one for that last one, and what if somebody had parked you in? Seriously, isn't it weird to not have that?"

"Yes. We had one lined up, but Odin spooked on him at the last minute, and Odin has a certain intuition, as you've no doubt noticed. Anyway, we'd been watching your bank long enough to feel confident about our timing."

"That's one bank."

"I know, I know. Sorry, sister, whether you drive tomorrow or not, we're releasing you blindfolded at a truck stop in Nevada, and you'll wander into the restaurant and have your fifteen minutes of fame."

"That sounds so delightful."

He sighed.

"What about my cut of the money?" I couldn't believe how bank robberish I sounded.

"We'll buy up a bunch of Paris Hilton quilts you won't have to deliver on. Zeus has it all worked out."

Zeus had it all worked out.

My heart sank.

"I want to stay with you guys," I said. "I want to stay Isis."

Thor frowned and pointed right. "Wanting doesn't make things happen."

I turned right. I had a feeling the test was over.

Chapter Eighteen

Thor and I ran a few actual errands. We got new sexy underwear for me that involved a corset and garter belt, plus straps, stockings, and even new shoes. And underwear for him. We also picked up new disposable phones, a wig, and finally, the sandwiches. Then we brought the car back to the hotel and parked it in the spot where it had been, and we took the elevator up to our floor.

It was after lunch. Odin and Zeus would be casing the bank for hours yet. So Thor and I watched *My Cousin Vinny*. After that, Thor took a dip in the hot tub with one of his mystery paperbacks while I read the paper.

After I got bored of that, I asked Thor if he thought it might be a good time for me to try on my new underwear. See if it all fit.

He gave me a heated look over the top of the pages. I took that as a *yes*.

I grabbed the shopping bags and headed to the nearest bedroom to change. My new black corset squished my breasts upward and together, my stockings were held up with clips that went to a belt under my corset, and my new high-heeled shoes matched the ensemble perfectly.

I loved how these new garments looked, and how they felt, too —all really complicated with ties and straps, but they left my pussy exposed.

I wished I could keep the things, but they were definitely impractical for a sheep farm.

I strolled out and stood over the hot tub. "What'dya think of the outfit?"

Thor stared at me for a spell. "Come here," he said in a husky way that told me he thought highly of the outfit.

I strolled over to the side. "I'm not getting in. I'm not getting this silk wet."

"It'll dry," Thor grated.

"You can't get this fabric wet. It gets misshapen."

"Really?"

I smiled. My badass Peter Pans, not understanding about laundry. They needed somebody like me. I so wished I could stay. "Do you guys ruin a lot of your clothes when you try to do washes?"

"Usually we get stuff washed for us or buy new."

"Possibly because you ruined your old stuff?" I asked.

"Was that a *no*?" he asked. "Are you changing the subject? Was that a no, that you're not getting in here?"

I swallowed. "That was a *no*," I said. "Because I care about these clothes."

His dark gaze roved over me lewdly.

Excitement pooled in my belly, in my bared crotch.

And he knew it.

We played well together, Thor and I, because he was so personable and talkative, but also off his chain.

"I like my new underwear," I said haughtily. "I'm not getting it wet."

He frowned.

My heart raced.

He stood up in the tub, all leisurely and powerful, water

running off his leanly muscled chest. He really did look like a god just then, wet and shining, but what really got me was the raw lust in his face.

He loved that I'd said I wouldn't get in. It was a ticket for him to be outrageous. What would he do? My heart fluttered in my throat as I stood there waiting.

He pointed to the table still strewn with breakfast stuff, and in his rough-smooth dirty talk voice, he said, "Go get the butter and bring it over here."

My belly warmed—at the request as much as the tone. "The butter?"

"Do it."

Was this leading up to a punishment? My sex clenched and I went over to get the butter. It got me hot just to walk a few yards to the table, knowing I was being watched—that was the erotic effect of that outfit.

And a simple command from Thor in that tone? And the fact that you never really knew what the mad doctor would do? This was fun already.

I brought the butter back and stood at the side of the hot tub, conscious of the cool air on my pussy, trying not to tremble with excitement. *Fuck me, punish me, use me*, I wanted to say.

"Put it down on the side of the tub and go turn on the jets." He pointed at the button.

I put the butter dish down and walked over to the wall button and pushed it. I went back and stood, feverishly awaiting my next command, but trying to look concerned, because that made it all more fun.

"Now, off with the shoes."

I kicked off my shoes.

"I thought you cared so much about your clothes, and here you kick off your shoes? Set them somewhere nice, like you care."

This command required more erotic walking, as well as some

erotic bending, which I did with total attitude. When I got back, I could see from his expression that he was quite moved by my show. It was such a turn-on to see him turned on. And it turned him on, I thought, to see me turned on.

If we kept going at this rate, one of us would have a heart attack.

"The stockings now," he grated. "And the corset, if it's so damn precious to you."

I pulled off my stockings and corset and draped them nicely over a chair, trembling clear down to my core.

His gaze was a leaden thing on my skin, cool and heavy.

"Now you have to put the shoes back on," he said, almost pleading, losing the whole commanding vibe.

I did it, of course. I walked back over and stood at the edge of the hot tub, looking down into the water. Would he not make me get in after all?

"Okay," he said. "Now kneel on the edge, facing away from me. On your hands and knees."

Erp. Things were full-on outrageous now.

I did it, kneeling on the smooth, warm marble, hands down. He came near me, drizzled water over my bare ass, letting it drip into my crotch. My whole body felt electric.

"Do you think I'm going to spank you?" he asked, drawing a wet finger up from my sensitive cleft to my asshole. I gasped as it tightened under his touch.

The notion *had* crossed my mind, though spanking seemed more Odin's area of interest than Thor's. But Thor voicing it now sent an anxious flutter through my belly. I'd had other ideas of what he was going to do, considering the butter delivery, but Thor could multitask.

"Do you?"

"No, I don't know what you'll do," I panted.

He dribbled some more water on me. It ran down my ass and

thighs in rivulets that cooled and tickled as they went. I wondered if he could see how slick my sex was, chilling in the air.

Really, Thor could do anything, and I would probably let him. The keyword there was do, though—I needed him to *do something*.

"You like not knowing."

"God, yes," I whispered. "And no."

"There's only one way to find out. Put your head down. Ass more in the air."

I did it, pressed my forearms to the smooth surface and my head between them. Again his warm hand roved over my butt cheeks. In this position, even more air was hitting the slickness between my legs, hitting my sensitive bud, heightening the nerves there until even the lightest touch of Thor's finger felt unbearably electric.

"I might spank you," he said. "But not right away."

OMG.

"Okay."

"You so want to fuck, you would let me do anything right now," he observed, practically reading my mind.

"Within reason," I said.

Without warning, his hand landed on my butt cheek with vicious force.

I gasped.

He slapped me again—hard.

And *again*.

I shut my eyes, giving myself over to the dark, delicious tremor of it.

"Anything," he said. "Your body is mine to do anything with. Until you say the word. Repeat it," he said. "My body..."

Oh! Thor had entered a new realm of dirty talk.

I hesitated and he spanked me again, vibrating my cheek and pussy in painful pleasure-tinged waves.

I hissed out a breath between my teeth, pressing my thighs together, feeling like just a little pressure would make me come at this point. *Just a little...*

"Oh, no, you don't—" He pushed one of my knees to the side, forcing me to spread my legs. "You're not going there without me. If you want satisfaction, you're going to say it. Anything..."

"Anything," I gasped. "My body is yours to do anything with. Anything you want, Thor, until I say the word. Please!"

"That's better."

I had this impulse to laugh from sheer excitement, but I knew not to. I heard the scrape of ceramic on marble.

The butter. "Ready?"

"For what?"

In his rough, silky voice, he said, "Whatever I want to do to you."

I don't know if it was his words that hypnotized me or the dirtiness of the garter belt with the shoes or the spanking or what, but I was feral with excitement. "Do whatever," I gasped. "Anything."

"Good girl." I felt his finger painting the butter over my asshole, up and down, and then more, slippery and silky and sensuous. He got more butter.

"Yes," I whispered.

Then I felt the tip of his finger push into my quivering asshole. And then farther. He pushed his finger in way deeper than he had in the car. I sighed, or more a kind of sigh-moan.

"Relax," he whispered, pressing farther. "Just relax." He got up a little rhythm and I moaned happily.

Then he pulled his finger out.

"Sit down now," he said. "Don't turn around, just sit down."

I sat cross-legged, ass on the cold marble. He took me around the waist, pulled me backward, slowly, into the water.

"What are you doing?"

"Shhh," he said into my hair. "Do you really give a fuck about those shoes anymore? Or that belt thing? Do you?"

"No," I said as my ass hit the water. But he didn't pull me all the way in, just halfway, so that my calves were resting on the side of the pool and the rest of me was in the water, except my head and shoulders. He held me there with his arms around my stomach.

Water shot out from a jet on the side, shooting toward me. Thor put his hand over my pussy and moved me to the right, pushing me forward, and when he took his hand away, the water was pulsing right into my clit, like a mega-vibrator.

"Lord have mercy," I hissed. It was almost too much pleasure.

"Feel it. Let it take you, let me take you."

"Fuck!" I said.

"Relax, give yourself over." And then he pressed his finger into my asshole, which was still buttery, and I began to pant and move with the sensation overload—the pulsing jets on my pussy, his finger sliding in and out of my ass.

His finger moved and curled in me now, as I was being thoroughly invaded and pleasured by the pulsating water.

I was breathing nearly in moans—I sounded like a bear! I made myself stop.

"Don't stop," he said huskily. "Give in. Give everything up to me. You have no choice."

The pleasure of his finger and the jets twisted in waves, in pulses, so relentlessly. The goodness of it filled me, and in a blink of an eye, I felt my orgasm building and I shattered apart with a cry, throbbing with feeling.

He pulled me back away from the jets as my climax subsided. Everything was fuzzy.

"Okay," he said. "I have to take you." He yanked me all the way in and hoisted me into his arms and kissed me. "I need to..." He was panting. "Come on." He carried me up the hot tub steps, out of the water, and across the suite, both of us dripping.

"Do me, fuck me any way you want," I said, kissing him as he carried me. He banged my feet into a wall.

"Sorry," he said.

"I'm not sorry." I could've lost half my leg and not cared at that point. He carried me the rest of the way down the hall and threw me down on the bed. He went up on his knees, cock erect, watching me wildly. He really did seem a bit wild, actually.

I rolled over and grabbed a condom from the nightstand and turned back to him, but before I could open it or put it on him, I just went to him and took his cock in my mouth, clutching his butt cheeks hard, taking him all the way to the back of my throat.

"Baby!" he said.

I sucked and tongued him creatively, then I gripped the base of his cock nice and hard and did him with my mouth and hand at the same time. He thrust into me, over and over. Then, with an almost animal force, he grabbed my hair and pulled me off him. He didn't have to say it twice.

Not even once.

I ripped open the condom and put it on him. Then I lay back and let myself be an offering to him, spreading my legs wide to him —I cared about nothing right then, nothing but being taken completely.

He stayed there on his knees, watching me, like part of the fucking was to just revel in the look of me, submitting utterly to him.

It was a very wonderful part of the fucking—being so turned on and knowing he was coming to me.

And then, with a stormy expression, the look of a man not in full possession of his senses, he crawled over me, all six-foot-whatever of muscular testosterone. He positioned the head of his fat cock into my opening, guiding himself just so, and drove in.

I sucked in a breath. He was so huge; it was this intense sensation with him, heading just to the edge of pain. I loved how it felt, the surprise of driving fullness.

He pulled out and drove in again.

"I can't stop," he said, ramming into me hard, again and again. "I can't stop, Ice, I feel like..."

"Then don't," I said, reveling in the intensity of being pounded by this thoroughly out-of-control man. "Fuck me, take me. Just...fuck me."

He drove into me relentlessly, and then a cry wrenched out of him, wrenched out the feeling from the depths of him. He stilled, cock pumping inside me, then he collapsed on me, panting.

I held him against me, one hand on his back, one on his hair, held his head to my shoulder.

He panted heavily, like he'd run for miles. It was the loudest sound in the hush of our suite.

I held him, wondering how he'd become this guy. Who he'd lost, what he'd lost. A *criminal*, he called himself, with hate and anger. But he'd once been a doctor.

"Fuck me, take me, just fuck me," he said. "Somebody needs dirty talk practice."

"Fuck the fuck off!" I pushed him away.

He laughed.

Chapter Nineteen

ODIN AND ZEUS CAME BACK LATE THAT AFTERNOON. They were thrilled with the catfish sandwiches, which were apparently a delicacy for bank robbers. They seemed unalarmed by Thor's having stolen a car for us to drive on errands, though I couldn't help but notice that Thor didn't tell them about the driving-in-front-of-a-cop-while-orgasming caper.

Was that whole incident really just another way an outlaw acts like an outlaw? Not important enough to mention?

Or was it something he preferred to hide?

Odin and Zeus talked about their day. They were feeling good about what they'd seen—roads, alarm company, security, routine.

Zeus said, "What really gets my dick hard is the way Odin's traffic light disruptors work."

"We took control of a light just on a drive by," Odin said. "*Fucking-g* thing of beauty."

"Lucky we didn't blow them on the Baylortown job." Thor tilted his head at me, eyes twinkling. "Oh, right, there aren't traffic lights there."

I hit him. He caught my wrist and kissed my hand.

We feasted and drank a lot that night, the four of us. Room

service carts were wheeled in and wheeled out; hot tub baths were taken. It was quite the drunken bash.

After about my fifth glass of champagne, I decided to model more of my new underwear, happy I'd saved most of it from a bath.

Zeus acted aloof about my getup—he was in some kind of strange, smoldery mood, but Odin took one look at me and slowly took off his glasses, which got me wild, as usual. He stood and stalked toward me.

I backed away until I hit a corner.

He kept coming until he mashed right into me.

It really was a kind of dance with these guys, and I loved every step of it. Odin trapped my hands above my head in the corner, mauling me deliciously, then he picked me up and brought me into another bedroom and we fucked, with Thor playing a fabulous supporting role.

Afterwards I noticed the tattoos on both their ankles.

"What is that? Clouds and lightning?" I asked, squinting as Odin pulled his pants back on.

"It's nothing. Let's get back to Zeus," Odin commanded.

I liked that they had matching tattoos, but I could see they didn't want me making a big deal out of it. I jumped up and quickly changed back into everybody's favorite sundress.

We went back out to find Zeus smoking a joint, dancing all by himself to *Kiss*—yes, the Prince song. He'd used this interlude to put together a special playlist. Thor and Odin joined him in the dancing.

I watched the three of them, filled with a kind of awe, thinking that when guys can dance around to an oldie like Prince with total abandon and still seem powerful and dangerous, they really have reached the far end of the tough-guy spectrum.

These were my kind of bank robbers.

"Come on," Thor called.

I jumped up and joined them. We danced while drinking champagne straight from the bottle. I was so getting into this outlaw thing.

An Elton John song came on. I put on my new wig of long brown hair—Thor and I had picked it up thinking about the heist—and it gave me the opportunity to swing my hair to the music, a pleasure I'd lost when we'd cut mine off.

The next song was *Beat It* by Michael Jackson. We all four danced like wild people. My bandits even seemed to know most of the words.

I got up and danced on the coffee table, and then Thor took his turn to do a special dance on the table, and then Odin did a strange sort of athletic dance later. We were all laughing. Even grumpy Zeus laughed a bit, though he refused to get up on the table and dance, much as we all begged.

I sighed, thinking it was so sad, Zeus not dancing to the oldies or taking part in our dirty fun. I eyed the latest set of flowers he had destroyed, petals ripped in half and left in little mounds near the vase, which contained only stems. Apparently not all the room service waiters had gotten the memo about bringing flowers to our room.

It made me want to cry.

Then again, I was very drunk.

Later, the subject was robbery. "It's ninety percent nerve," Thor said to me after the waiter had delivered a cart with a pyramid of chocolate candies. "Bank robbery is ninety percent nerve, and the nerve makes the magic."

I teased him about being new age-y. A new age bank robber. That almost got me a spanking punishment, but it was quickly commuted to the withholding of chocolates. I took some anyway and we wrestled around, fighting over them, and eventually Zeus threw Thor in the hot tub. My badass Peter Pans were all about the decadent criminal lifestyle.

The next day we were all hungover and subdued.

Odin and Zeus did a bit more surveillance, and there were some practice runs.

That night, the eve of the robbery, my bandits behaved like monks. They ate healthy meals and went to bed early without sex. They pulled into themselves, each in their own way, marshaling their inner reserves.Something Zeus said made me think that this was their usual pattern—a night of wildness two nights before a robbery to blow off steam, but a night of good behavior right before the robbery.

Suddenly it was the next day, and we were on our way to knock off another First City.

Thor had convinced them to let me babysit the car outside the bank, swearing up and down I had the nerve for it. Zeus was weird about it, like there was something voodoo about me taking Venus's place as car sitter, even temporarily.

But really, what if somebody double parked and screwed up their escape?

He relented.

They were such pros in so many ways, but when you lifted the corners, they were all a little bit wounded.

I knew how they were going to pull it off—the four of us had had a lot of discussions about First City procedures and I felt like I'd really helped them refine their ideas. It would be a cinch, but still, I was pretty apprehensive.

Thor stole a different car for the job—an old Thunderbird—and not from the hotel parking lot. The idea was that we'd ditch it and switch to the van on the other side of town; the van was waiting for us, all tricked out with compartments.

So there I was, driving my guys in a stolen car, wearing the brown wig over my short platinum hair, and gloves, of course, because my fingerprints were on file, being that I'd been in the banking industry. I had my own throwaway phone in my pocket. I felt like a real bank robber.

When they'd robbed my bank, they'd blown up two cars and set smoke bombs, creating chaos to aid their getaway.

This time, they were going for the traffic light chaos—Odin had created little electronic impulse-emitting devices for placement on stoplights to throw the timing off. He'd jogged around town putting them on there at dawn. They'd also messed with the back parking lot cameras.

They wore their fine business suits, and Thor put on the earpiece that let him monitor police communications. I let them off in different areas—Zeus would go in alone first, then Thor and Odin would go in together afterward with Starbucks cups as their props, like colleagues out for a midmorning coffee run.

After I dropped them off, I drove around the block once, as we'd practiced the day before, and pulled into one of the secluded spots in the back, almost in an alley.

We'd identified this place ahead of time.

I let the back door hang open an inch so that it would be easy for Thor and Odin to get in. I positioned myself between the seats in the front so that I could slam into the passenger side quickly and let Zeus take the wheel, but I'd still have access to the driver's side if I needed to maneuver the car for any reason.

I was to call if I saw cops. I was ready with my phone, number plugged in.

I would be such a good partner to them! But it would be bad if I could never go home. That was not something I wanted.

I waited, heart pounding, engine running.

A few bank customers went in the back way—most FCNs have front and back entrances.

They'd estimated the robbery would take seven minutes.

Right around minute eight, I started freaking out. No cops entered, and I heard no gunshots, but a lot can go wrong in a robbery. Never had I realized quite how much could go wrong, in fact, until I was sitting there thinking of all the ways.

And then the door flew open, and my three guys came walking out—fast—carrying bags, wearing their masks.

I opened the driver's side door and slid into the passenger side. Zeus buckled up and they all tore off their masks and we were off, gunning through the alley and out onto the street.

"A second robbery. That should result in some fucked-up publicity for your old boss," Odin said. "And you're going to be happy with our take."

Thor said, "Very happy, Ice."

"Sounds to me like some naughty tellers weren't keeping their second drawers light," I said.

Zeus rolled down the window. Cars jammed the streets, honking, but mostly the routes *to* the bank were affected. They'd chosen the Thunderbird for its pickup. If we had to run, it would be in the Thunderbird.

We rolled out of the business district, not talking. I had this feeling it was too easy, but I didn't want to jinx things by saying that aloud.

We parked around the corner from the van—illegally, but hey, that's the luxury of a stolen car—and got out with the money in bags and briefcases.

We headed into a department store, splitting up inside—Thor and I pretended to be a couple out shopping, looking at shoes; Odin and Zeus wandered around on their own.

This, too, we'd practiced the day before.

The entire escape plan was completely different from the one they'd used with my bank. My guys seemed far more worried about anybody making a connection from one bank job to another than about outwitting the cops on any single job.

It made me so sad to think that after this I'd be dumped in a truck stop in Nevada while blindfolded. Furthermore, Thor had told me we'd have to fuck up my haircut, otherwise people would know it was professionally done. "If your story is that we kept you blindfolded and drugged most of the time, your hair has to look like we cut it ourselves," he said.

At least I got to keep the color—the stylist had left a bit of roots. The hair color version of pre-ripped jeans.

Out the corner of my eye, I saw Zeus heading for the door that led to the street the van was on. Then Odin.

"They're out," I said.

Thor took my hand and we wandered toward the exit, out onto the sidewalk, and into the back of the van. Zeus and Odin were in the front, as usual.

We headed out to the highway, took a curlicue, and hit I-59 going northwest.

The mood loosened once we were zooming along.

Odin boasted about what *fucking-g* awesome robbers they were, one of his favorite hobbies.

Thor counted up the money. Let's just say many Paris Hilton comforters would soon be ordered.

That's when the trouble started.

Chapter Twenty

At first it was just Zeus not liking a car behind us. Evidently, it's hard to tell if a car is following you on the highway; the only way is to slow down or take an exit.

Zeus slowed.

The suspicious car slowed.

That got everyone's attention.

My stomach twisted in knots. "You think it's the cops?"

"No," Zeus said ominously.

Oh. The *other* guys. The ones they were *actually* scared of.

Odin and Thor argued about taking the upcoming exit. They pulled out their phones, scanning special maps that I didn't have on my phone.

Odin suggested the exit after. It was a better place for bailing, he thought. There was a flea market. An antique car show event next to it. Some kind of fairgrounds that would be good and busy.

"Fuck if we're bailing," Zeus said, but he took the exit.

So did our tail.

Thor sucked in a deep breath, sat straight, belted in. "Put your wig back on, Ice," he said.

As if on cue, Zeus took a violent U-turn and then gunned the engine.

"Crap!" I grabbed the door handhold, shoving on my wig.

Thor continued, unperturbed by the car chase. "Zeus can probably outrun this guy, but you may need to bail with us. You can't let them catch you. And you have a good chance to get away, because it won't be you they're focusing on. It's us they want."

I gripped the handhold more tightly as the van careened around a corner. "Can I help? If it's not me they want?"

"No. And don't try. It's better for all of us." We swung around another corner, tires screeching. "Don't look out there," Thor said. "Look at me and try to relax."

"Are you saying that because I'll have less chance of being injured in a car crash if I'm not tensed?"

"Yes," Thor said. "That's kind of why."

"What? But telling me that counteracts it, right?"

He grinned sadly. Was he just trying to distract me?

"How bad is this?"

"Do we have skills?" he asked.

"They must've staked out the van," Odin said from the front as Zeus sped up ominously. "This isn't even the robbery, it's the goddamn van."

"What I wouldn't give for those fuckin' eight cylinders in that T-bird, goddammit," Zeus growled, turning again, practically tipping us over.

"*Fucking-g* American pussy van," Odin muttered.

"I don't want us to die in a car," I said.

"You won't." Thor grabbed my hand. "If we bail, you just concentrate on getting out of sight and finding a hidey hole. Then you ditch that jacket and that wig and forget about us. Remember our story? You've been drugged and blindfolded for two or three days."

"Right." I nodded.

"You don't know how long it's been," Thor continued, "and you don't want to talk. Remember how we talked about how you don't have to say shit?"

I nodded. I didn't have to say shit.

I couldn't believe this might be the end for us.

I wanted to say something poignant to Thor, to all of them. I wanted to tell them how amazing they were. I wanted to say what they meant to me.

I didn't know how to put it into words.

It was huge, what they meant to me. Maybe too huge. They'd shaken my life out of its stupor. But it was more. They'd shown me that home could be many different things.

I wanted so badly to stay, but this was starting to look like goodbye.

The ride turned bumpy, like we were going over railroad ties or something. Or maybe it was the van.

Odin said, "There's a DD south of the city. That's our meet-up spot. On the sevens at the seven."

"What's a DD?" I asked frantically.

"I can't tell you that," Thor said. "That is a code about where we're meeting later. We're probably going to have to split up, Ice, and you can't know. For your own good."

"Right," I whispered, heart breaking.

"Breathe," Thor commanded. And then he gave me a hug.

I clung onto him shamelessly for a split second, and then it was back to business. We were in danger. That had to be the focus now.

"Odin likes the fairgrounds," Thor said. "A trade show, a car show, it's a fucking rabbit warren. We can do this. *You* can do this. You're going to get back to your nice life after this. And we'll buy up your silly Paris Hilton comforters."

"I don't care about the comforters," I said.

"Entering fairgrounds. Get ready!" Odin called out.

"Looks like you'll never get to see us in kilts, but I know you'll imagine it." Thor squeezed my hand. "I go first."

They'd done this before. They all seemed to know their parts. "Okay? You stay until Zeus tells you."

"Good luck..." I said, baffled. "Thank you..."

Thor jammed some money and a bunch of other stuff into his pockets and strapped on a fanny pack. He stretched a fist out toward Zeus and Odin. "God Pack," he said

Zeus and Odin clasped his fist, making one large fist out of all of their hands.

It was so poignant, my three robbers in danger, clamping onto each other. "Come on, Ice," he said.

I set my small hand on their fist-and-hand conglomeration, trying not to cry.

This really was goodbye, then.

The van screeched and slowed. Thor jumped out into a crowd and we surged forward again, almost running over some people.

I stared in horror out the back window. Somebody got out of the car behind us and dashed into the crowd.

"They're following him!" I said.

"They won't catch him," Odin growled.

We screeched around a tent, off-roading now. People screamed.

Zeus zoomed into a parking ramp and started racing around, climbing upwards.

"This is screwed up!" Odin said. He and Zeus argued about how to shake the tail. Odin had firecrackers he thought to use.

It was all happening so fast—all this danger on the heels of the suspense and the debauchery.

I finally understood what Thor meant about why everything had to be so extreme—the luxury, the food, the sex. Everything too much and all at once, but it all balanced out in a weird way.

We headed back down.

I was completely dizzy by the time we blasted out of the ramp onto a relatively empty straightaway behind a building. Cars and semi-trailer trucks lined the sides.

"Bye, Isis," Odin said with a deep gaze into my eyes that seemed to contain a world of longing and significance.

Zeus slowed.

Odin jumped out, right out from the moving van, rolling on the ground and then dashing between trucks and disappearing.

Zeus and I kept on. Or more, we bumped on. Something was wrong with the van.

"We're riding the rims," Zeus said. "Just like we're on an episode of COPS, huh?"

"That's not incredibly comforting," I said.

We headed behind a main fairgrounds building, but the van was breaking down. Slowing, bumping harder.

"See those workers going in and out of the back of that long building?" Zeus asked. "We're going near there. When I say the word, you pop out and run like hell for that door, got it? You get in there and make your way through to the front of the building where the crowds are. It's probably a storage area or a kitchen back here, but it will lead to the front. Just use your will. Once you're through, into the public part, you go left and get lost, got it? Once you're in there, you do not know me."

"Got it." It was all happening too fast.

Zeus seemed to have more to say. "I'm sorry," he said.

"Don't apologize."

"Ready? You'll have to go while this thing is moving. I'm behind you, but don't worry about me. Just make it in there. See it? Can you do it?"

"I can do it."

"You don't know me," he said again. Maybe he was right. Maybe I never really did know him. And I never would.

We slowed, maybe ten yards from the back service entrance of a giant event building.

"Now!" he said.

I took one last look into his haunted green eyes.

"Go."

I jumped out and fell, then I got up and ran for the door. A man in an apron tried to stop me. He held me by the arms. "Where's your badge?"

A crash of metal and glass sounded behind me.

Suddenly Zeus was there. He yanked the guy sideways onto the ground and we ran in to some sort of food storage area.

We headed into a kitchen. Workers in painters' whites stared at us.

We continued through and out into a cavernous event space filled with people and booths and cars and music.

Part of the car show, I thought.

We got some dirty looks for coming in the wrong entrance.

"Go!" Zeus pointed left.

I went left and stole around a booth, legs like rubber. I wove in and out of booths until I was lost.

Once I was certain I wasn't being followed, I ducked into the women's bathroom and slipped into a stall.

I pulled off my coat and wig and stuffed them into the sanitary napkin disposal bin.

Okay, I thought. *Free*.

Or was I? I eyed the window high on the wall. What if I climbed out of it? But then I might look more guilty.

I heard women come in and out. I used the toilet and flushed it, then went out and washed my hands, pulse racing.

Could the entrance be staked out?

Thor had said they wouldn't care about me. With trembling hands, I fixed my hair and tucked my shirt into my jeans.

Then I steeled myself and walked casually out onto the event center floor.

Nothing happened. Just a lot of people.

I wandered around, looking at the old cars, feeling naked without a purse, and just really alone—more alone than I'd ever felt. I suppose because nobody in the world knew where I was. I could so easily disappear. I wondered how my guys were faring. I closed my eyes, sent them each a good thought.

It was near the 1950s trucks area that I saw the knot of people. Something happening. I wandered over and pushed in a ways—just enough to see Zeus, lying motionless on the concrete floor.

I tried to keep myself composed, like I was just another person. "What happened? Was he shot?" I asked the woman next to me.

"Shot? No." She looked at me funny, like, why would I think that? "He collapsed, looks like."

Three men in street clothes were hoisting him up onto a stretcher, and I was pretty sure they weren't doctors. Two EMTs stood on the sidelines, looking bewildered and angry. "Why aren't the EMTs helping him?"

She shrugged.

I felt frantic. Had the bad guys forced the EMTs to relinquish their stretcher? I turned to the woman. "The EMTs brought that stretcher?"

She nodded, brows knit.

"And those guys took over?"

Another nod.

I had to act fast; they were preparing to carry Zeus off, and it probably wasn't anywhere good.

I pushed in without thinking. "I'm a nurse. Let me help."

"It's under control." A man with pale pinkish skin and a crew cut lifted the front end. A thick-necked guy had the back and another with gray hair stood by.

"Did you get his vitals?" I asked.

"It's under control." They began to carry him toward the back. I had to do something!

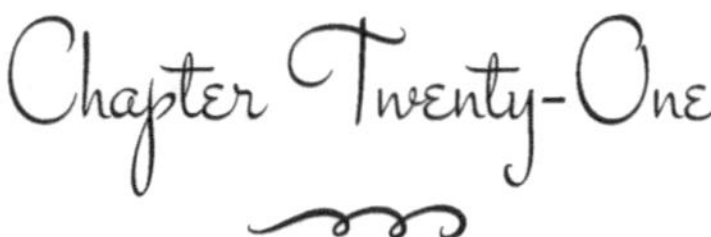

Chapter Twenty-One

I FOLLOWED. "WHERE ARE YOU TRANSPORTING HIM TO? What medical center?" My lines were coming completely from TV at this point.

They ignored me as they passed into the kitchen and I just followed them, right out through and to the back, the way we'd come in. What could they do to me around all these people? Though there weren't so many once we were outside.

Our trashed van was still out there, nose smashed into a parked truck. The men set down the stretcher next to a large black Lincoln Navigator and hoisted Zeus up by the arms.

"You can't do that!" I said. "He might have a spinal injury! I demand to see your credentials."

They ignored me, stuffing him into the back seat.

"You can't just transport a man like this!" I protested.

A hand grabbed my hair. Something hard poked into my back.

A gun.

"Get in."

"Leave her," the thick-necked man said.

"What do the two numbers on a blood pressure reading signify?" the man with the gun asked me.

I didn't know the answer. But did they? "Baseline and high-point," I bluffed.

"Wrong. In." Rough hands shoved me into the back seat next to Zeus. The thick-necked guy squeezed in next to me and we were off.

"What is this?" I demanded.

"You fucking up, that's what this is," the pale man said from the front. "You showing us you're with him."

"You can't do this!"

And then the thick-necked one punched me in the face.

The blow snapped my head back.

"One more word and you die in here," he said.

I gaped at him, ears ringing, mouth filling with the taste of blood. The punch stunned me so much, my thinking felt as jumbled as my face. I looked over at Zeus—I could see from the rise and fall of his chest that he was still breathing. Had he been hurt? Drugged?

The thick-necked guy made me empty my pockets and clean out Zeus's. I pretended not to find his cell phone.

"Your friend's trail of ripped flowers wasn't so hard to follow," he said triumphantly.

I pretended not to hear or care, but I hated that they might've used what I'd come to regard as Zeus's expression of grief to find him and Thor and Odin.

We rode in silence, except for my heart thundering like a bongo. My mind raced in circles—what to do, how to get out. Maybe twenty minutes later we stopped in some kind of shipping yard. The pale guy with the crew cut pulled Zeus out and found the cell phone.

For that, the thick-necked guy hit me again. It was more stunning the second time, and I began to cry.

I backed up and the older guy grabbed me by the hair and started forcing me toward a gray metal boxcar, the sort you'd see on a freight train, except it was on the ground. More box than boxcar.

The blond man unlocked a padlock and swung open the door. The guys shoved the two of us in. Then they shut it back up and locked it.

And it was completely dark inside.

I crawled across the metal floor, feeling for Zeus, finding his leg, feeling up to his face. I cupped his cheek. "Zeus," I whispered. "Zeus!"

He didn't answer. I shook him gently. From what I could feel, he was in a twisted position. Was something broken? I laid him out straight, on his back, wishing I could see him, see if he had injuries.

I crawled to the door and put my ear to it. I could hear nothing. I felt around until I found a handle, and I yanked and pushed and rattled, but there was no budging it.

It was an inky-black sensory deprivation chamber in there, and way hot, too. It came to me that it might be airtight, though it had looked rusty on the outside. Where there was rust, there were holes, right?

Just no light, I told myself.

Just don't breathe a lot, I told myself.

I went back to Zeus and stretched out beside him. The sound of his breathing comforted me.

"Zeus," I whispered now and then, but he never stirred. I sometimes put my fingers to his neck to feel his pulse. I also took off his shoes and socks, and I put his socks under his head as a pathetic little cushion. I wanted to take off more just so he'd stay cool, but I didn't want to bang his body around in case he was injured.

I don't know how much time passed, though I know the sun was beating down on us, because the air got hotter and thinner in our container—like a sauna. I was starting to feel like I couldn't breathe.

Nothing but panic, I told myself.

I heard rumbling nearby at one point and I banged on the wall and yelled, but nobody came to investigate. Afterwards, I collapsed on my knees, faint from the effort. I wasn't entirely sure my mind was working right.

Well, they hadn't killed us. Did that mean they had a use for us? Would they come back when Zeus awoke? And what then?

I stretched back out next to Zeus, monitoring his breathing, like if I didn't pay attention, he might stop. I don't know how many hours had passed when he finally grunted.

"Zeus!" I kneeled, put a hand on his forehead. "Zeus! Wake up!"

Nothing.

I shook him and lightly slapped his cheeks. "Zeus!"

He defended himself drunkenly, pushing weakly at my arms. "What'reyadoing?" he mumbled, running the words together.

"Zeus," I said. "It's me! Wake up!"

He said nothing more. I massaged his hands. "Come on!" Then I massaged his shoulders, his arms, getting the blood flowing. Since he'd clearly been drugged, maybe extra blood flow would be good.

"Whererewe?" he said.

"I don't know. Some sort of sealed container, like a locked metal box. I think this is the railroad yard, but maybe not. It's so hot, I feel like there's no air! Sorry, I don't mean to alarm you, though." That wasn't constructive. I forced myself to concentrate through the heat and the dizziness, to describe everything I knew in complete detail. We could put our heads together.

He was silent for a long time more, then, "Whererewe?"

Okay, he hadn't gotten any of that.

Crap.

I rested my forehead on his chest, feeling dizzy. The sweat poured out of me. I wanted to cry.

Deep down, I knew our predicament wasn't like on Batman or something where Batman and Robin would be tied on some contraption that they could escape from. Real-life bad guys didn't do that.

We were in real trouble. The men who'd put us here were dangerous enough to strike fear into the hearts of my very capable criminals.

And it was hard to breathe. The too-hot air felt painful inside my throat and lungs...that couldn't be good. In fact, it seemed dangerous. The more I thought about it, the more freaked I got.

We could boil to death. Our insides would be jelly!

I shook Zeus some more—violently. I was officially freaking out. "You *have* to wake up!"

Nothing.

I put my head to his chest and began to sob. Suddenly I felt his arms come around me. He held me tightly. "You're here...can't believe you're here!" His voice sounded thick, words slurred. Then, "I'm sorry, I'm so, so sorry, baby. I can't believe you're here."

"I couldn't just leave," I said. "I couldn't leave you like that."

"Why?" he grated out. "Why'd you leave?"

I pressed my face to his chest, confused. He'd *instructed* me to leave. Walk left and get lost, he'd said.

"Why?" he grumbled out in the darkness. "Did you give one thought...one thought...to those you left behind?"

I felt drugged by the heat, by the pitch-black darkness. His words made me think about my sisters. *What about us? Why did you leave us?*

"Did you even think of that?" he asked.

Was he talking about my sisters?

"Did you?" he pressed.

"Of course I did!" I said. "You think I don't care? I know that's what you think, and you couldn't be more wrong." I began to cry. I wouldn't see my sisters again. "Fuck!" I said.

"Shh, I'm sorry. I'm sorry." He smoothed a hand over my hair, which amounted to matting it down because it was so utterly wet with sweat. "God, I've been so lonely without you. I couldn't believe you were gone. You were there with us, and then you were gone."

He thinks I'm Venus.

He was talking to Venus.

"I'm sorry," he continued. "I controlled you. Suffocated you. It's my fault."

Naturally his words made me think about the message on the site. *We miss you, we suffocated you. Things will be different.* I'd left my poor sisters behind to suffer, to blame themselves. I'd never get a chance to tell them it wasn't their fault.

It's just that I'd found something I'd been looking for.

"I'm so sorry," he continued.

Tears tickled my cheeks.

It was as if he was saying the part of my sisters.

The hot metal floor felt like it was tilting. I knew it was dizziness, but the tilting felt real. And the wires in my head were getting crossed. Reality and unreality twisted into a pretzel.

I said, "I wanted what I wanted." I felt like I was talking to Vanessa and Kaitlin and Candy. Like I was saying my last words to them.

I said, "It wasn't about you controlling me or suffocating me—I just needed to leave. I wish I could've told you. Made you understand. I needed to be free!"

"Not like this!" he said.

"Yes, like this," I said hazily. "You need to get that! You have to forgive yourself!" It was everything I'd wished I could've typed on that blog post comment. My need to say these words to my sisters felt urgent, like the only thing that mattered.

"I was selfish," he said. "I pushed you."

"Nobody was pushing anybody," I said hazily.

He shifted around there on the hot metal floor in the darkness. I couldn't see him, but I felt his breath heave out, felt his big body in front of mine. I reached out and touched his face, discerning that he was lying on his side in front of me. He grabbed my shoulders and pressed his forehead to my chest, between my breasts. The heat seemed to intensify as I laid my hand onto the back of his head, holding him, pulling him fully to me.

"I didn't want you to go," he said.

"You had no choice. We were all just surviving the best we could," I said. "But it's all okay now. You have to know that. It's all okay."

A harsh sob jolted his huge body, then another, and another— it was as if a floodgate opened in him. And this giant, powerful man was weeping.

Everything was wet—our sweat, tears, the air—reality itself seemed drenched. I felt as if I were breathing in his relief, taking it in great gulps.

"It's all okay. Don't be sad. You can let it go."

My sisters would never hear what I had to say, but I was saying the words nevertheless, and it shifted something in me. It was like I was saying my part to the universe. It felt like that counted in some strange way.

And Zeus hearing it counted for something, too. His being relieved counted for something.

"I would do it again," I said, holding him. "You needed what you needed. It wasn't your fault. We were all victims. I just needed to be free. And there's nothing to forgive. Do you understand?"

He seemed quiet. Peaceful. I knew that he understood.

The world inside our hot metal box seemed to be spinning, shifting. We were like two strange puzzle pieces, saying our parts to the universe.

Would we die now?

Zeus straightened, touched my hair. Then he touched my hair

differently, patting it. Not that gentle touch, but an angry touch. "Isis?"

"Yes," I said.

"Jesus! What the hell?" He pulled away from me. "What the hell? Where are we? Why are you pretending to be Venus?"

"I didn't mean...I wasn't..."

"What is wrong with you? Why would you do that?"

I frowned. No answer would make sense.

"Where the hell are we?" His questions echoed in the hot tin can.

I tried to explain where we were, but he was already up, exploring the walls from what I could hear. Pounding on them. Maybe kicking them.

"Son of a bitch," he said after one loud bang. "Son of a fucking bitch!" I wondered if he'd hurt himself. "And you're in here acting like you're Venus? Let me tell you something—you're not Venus."

"Yeah, I know I'm not Venus!" I said. "I think I got that."

"Then why were you pretending to be her? You come into our gang and you try to take her place, running all over trying to erase her tracks—"

"I wasn't trying to erase her tracks—"

"And now you're in here talking like you're her from the dead? You think it's funny to mess with me like that?"

"I wasn't trying to mess with you! Excuse me if I've been locked in a human-sized air fryer with you for five or ten hours and a little disoriented. Excuse me if you're completely checked out except when you're saying the stuff my sisters would say, who I'll probably never see again, who I feel guilty about leaving, contrary to your assessment of it. Excuse me if I have some weepy things to say back while being air-fried to death." I sounded incoherent, even to myself.

"You knew I thought you were Venus. You should've said something."

"Well, guess what? I barely know which way is up right now. And I was talking to my sisters. So screw off," I said.

"Trying," Zeus said.

I heard him move around the perimeter of our hell-cage. He rattled something on the side we'd come in.

"That would be the padlocked door," I said.

He rattled it some more.

"And I'll tell you something else," I continued. "I bet you she'd say the same stuff I was saying. You didn't make her kill herself, Zeus. Nobody can make somebody kill themselves. So you can get off your high horse. You're not a god."

The rattling stopped. I wished I could see his face. His eyes.

I said, "You may be the center of the universe in your mind, and you're the center of your pack, but you think you're so powerful that you can drive a person to suicide? People do what they want to do. She made her own choices, just like I did. Let her have that, Zeus. Let her have it!"

I heard his footsteps near me in the darkness. I sniffled as he sat beside me. Did he hate me for saying that? Maybe, but it's the sort of thing I'd have wanted my sisters to know.

I felt his heavy hand on my knee, my arm, fumbling upward for my shoulder where it rested.

Was he trying to be nice now? Was this hand on my shoulder supposed to be comforting?

"Hey," he said.

"What?"

"They just love you, that's all," he said. "Your sisters love you."

I felt my face crumple with tears. I didn't bother covering it, one of the few advantages of being in abject darkness. "I love them, too," I gasped out. "But I needed to be free, and I loved being free. I don't think they'll ever understand. Well, they sure won't now."

"Fuck, come here." He pulled me to him. I fought to get my sobs under control...without a lot of success.

He smoothed back my hair. "I understand," he said. Then, finally, "I'm sorry."

I sniffled. "Are you saying that to Venus or Isis?" I asked.

"Both," he said after a long silence. "I guess both. Are you okay with that?"

"Of course I am," I said. "Are you?"

He pulled away. I knew he was looking at me there in the dark. I could feel his gaze. The intensity of him. "You would've really said that to them? To your sisters?"

"Of course. Blaming themselves for a thing I did? It's just not right. On any level."

"But they pushed you. They made you stay, took too much from you. You said so once."

"They did that, but there are other responses than leaving and taking up with robbers. That was my choice, not something they made me do. Or jumping off a cliff. That was not Venus's only option."

His breath sounded ragged. Was he even listening?

"I don't want them to blame themselves," I added. "You shouldn't, either."

In the silence that followed, I wondered if I'd hurt or angered him.

"It helps me that you say that," he finally said.

Something in me relaxed. "It helps me that you understand."

He let out this breath, this labored exhale, as though he'd been holding it forever. "Okay, then," he said.

We sat there in silence that droned on and on.

Machinery sounded outside in the distance, then faded.

"Thanks," he said after a while.

"Back atcha." I felt strangely connected to him. And a little bit better, even. It was as though our guilty souls had been washed together.

I felt him sit up. He smoothed back my hair again. Drips of sweat rolled off my forehead, rolling along my hairline.

"We have to get the fuck out of here," he said.

"Where you were last, I'm pretty sure that was the door." I found his hand and pressed it to the floor, moving it in the direction of the door. "That way."

He crawled to the door side of our box. I heard him feeling around and banging at the metal. "I wish they hadn't taken my shoes."

"No, here!" I fumbled around until I found his shoes.

He put them on and banged at the door, presumably with his feet, trying to get it open. I didn't hear him peel off his shirt, but I heard the soft clop when he threw it. I put on my shoes, too, and fumbled my way over to him. We sat on our asses together in the darkness, ramming the door with our feet in unison until I thought my heel bones were cracked.

"No go," he said finally.

We collapsed back, side by side.

I wished I could see him. I thought back to that day at the bank, the way his eyes looked behind that mask, the connection I felt. I flashed on his gaze that day in the hot tub—all that hunger and disdain in his eyes, but still the intensity was there. The connection.

"I never meant to erase her tracks. I never wanted that."

"I know," he said.

We didn't talk about the air. I still wanted to believe there was a pinhole letting some in.

"I'm sorry to have pulled you into this."

"I said you shouldn't blame yourself."

"That *sorry* was for you, not her." A beefy finger slid across my wet forehead.

"Well...you get the same response. I chose it. So you can just respect that."

"Thank you."

"Anytime," I said.

Another breathy little laugh in the darkness. He moved closer. In spite of the heat, I liked touching him. I needed it. I snuggled into him, enjoying his calm—that calm of a large animal that he had.

I was enjoying his maleness, too.

He slid a hand down my arm. A sluice of sweat ran ahead of where he stroked, like he was pushing rivulets of sweat down to my wrist, wiping them right off me. Slick, everything slick. He shifted, then, and I sensed his face nearing mine in the darkness. Lightly, he kissed me on the cheek. Then he found my lips.

This wild swell of desire came over me as we kissed. I needed him like I'd never needed anybody.

"You are so beautiful," he whispered into the kiss.

I wiped the stinging sweat out of my eyes. "You probably say that to all the girls in a pitch-black death trap from which there's no hope of escape."

I really wanted him to say that there was hope of an escape. That he had a plan or at least some faith that we'd get out.

I waited in the silence that followed, but he didn't say any of that.

He didn't think we'd get out, either.

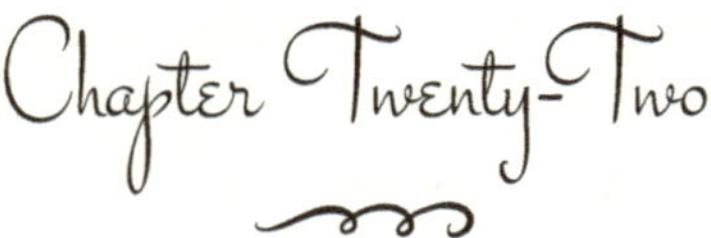

Finally, he spoke. "I don't say it to all the girls in a pitch-black death trap." He sounded serious now. "I say it to you. I always thought it. I thought it that first moment at the bank. I thought you were beautiful. Different."

I touched his soaked chest. I figured we would run out of sweat at some point, but for now we were slick fish in a strange pond.

Suddenly his lips came down on my neck. A jolt of lightning went through me. I snaked my hand over his shoulder, feeling so close to him, like we were porous to each other.

He kissed my neck, moved his lips to the base of my neck, that tender center part. His lips there felt as intimate as fucking. He kissed me on the lips then, cupping my cheeks.

"You know what it's been like?" he breathed. "Watching you with them?"

I snaked my hands around his chest, skin hot and slippery, feeling so connected to him now, like he was revealing his heart.

"When I saw you on the couch that first day with Thor and Odin, I wanted to tear you three apart," he said. "I hated them for bringing you in and having you take her place."

He was silent for a while. I could feel how hard it was for him to say it.

"It was so bad at the end with her in that downward spiral. No way to help her. I was cruel to her because I wanted her to shape up. Then suddenly she was dead. So it was this grief and guilt and relief, all mixed together. You know? Watching you three together, it made me feel twice as messed up about her. I wanted to join in, but I couldn't get past how I felt. You came and brought all this life to us, brought the feel of our family back. I wanted you so bad, but I hated you for stirring it all up again. Even then, though, I couldn't stop wanting to be with you, Ice."

I touched his cheek, grateful for that.

He slid his hand down my wet shirtfront. There were no words —just his touch.

I reached up to his chest, wanting to touch him everywhere, to be naked with him. "Be with me now," I said.

"Ice."

"Please," I whispered.

He let out a great, gusty breath and yanked open my soggy shirt. I heard buttons ping on corrugated metal.

I barked out a laugh, half surprise, half thrill.

"What the hell," he whispered, running his hands over my breasts. "We're rich bank robbers. We can buy all the shirts in the world."

I laughed. It shouldn't have been funny, but nothing mattered at that point.

I wrestled out of my pants—I couldn't get them off fast enough. I wanted to be under him, to be taken by him. I pushed him to the warm metal floor and pulled his pants off.

Dizziness came over me as I tossed them aside, but I didn't stop. I stroked his thighs, slippery with sweat, crawling up over him, slicking my hands up, up, up in the darkness until I reached his rock-hard, wet cock. I stroked him, loving touching him, so hot for him.

He groaned and rose, flipped me over, came over me, loomed over me as I stroked him. I had this thought he should stay lying, to conserve his energy.

But...*why?*

He growled and bit my neck, all wolfish, then licked and kissed and bit his way down to my breast, sucking, tonguing, as I wriggled under him, cock in hand, awash in sensation.

I lost contact with his cock as he moved his lower half out of my range, but there was so much more of him for me to touch and squeeze, and I did it, my hands roving all over his strong arms and shoulders, his chest.

I wanted to cry, that was how bad I wanted him. That was how grateful I felt that he was there with me, with his power and intelligence and big-animal calm.

Confident, heavy hands hydro-planed over my wet skin and my quivering belly, delving to my slick sex, fingers in my cunt, then back up, pushing up over my breasts and neck and inside my mouth. I sucked in his fingers, keeping them mine. I wanted to consume him inside and out, and for him to consume me.

Then I let his fingers go. "Do it," I panted.

There was this pause, then I felt him pushing my legs open.

I slid under him a bit, gripping his big shoulders. "Yes!"

He said, "I don't have—" He panted, "Don't have—" *Don't have a condom.*

I considered my cycle—I was in a pretty safe zone, and then I thought, why am I even worrying?

"Hello, we're being steamed like oysters," I said. "Be inside me, Zeus. Come inside me. Fuck me!"

He growled—a yes if I'd ever heard one. He set to kissing my belly, my breasts, rough last kisses, and then he guided his cock into me and plunged in with a guttural cry.

It was glorious to be filled by him, and so intense I thought I might black out. Or was that from the heat?

Actually, I may have for a second, but then I was back, and he was driving into me, slowly, sensuously, moaning softly with every thrust. I loved his man-moans, and the way his furred belly slid against my belly, and how his legs pressed along my legs.

I held him, moved with him.

Everything between us was so heated, so on the edge, it seemed unwise, yet I wanted it to last.

He drove into me and I gasped, feeling like I might pass out again.

Breathe normally! I told myself, but it was all too hot on every level. And it didn't matter.

He changed his angle and I cried out from the deliciousness of it, my voice echoing inside the box.

He fucked me new yet again, sending stars into my mind, tremors into my body. I was going delirious, like we might be fucking ourselves to death. It was a total God Pack way to die.

The sensation increased, and I grabbed onto his arms, then his back, digging into his skin for dear life as we fucked like wild bears. My hands were slipping all over. His skin felt slick. Had I drawn blood?

"I think I gouged you! I'm sorry," I gasped.

"What do I care? Take everything, Isis. Take it all." He came down closer, propped himself on his elbows and grabbed my hair as he pumped into me. "Take it all!" He kissed the breath out of me. I swung my legs around him, took him deep, getting pleasure fringed with pain.

I groaned as the orgasm uncoiled in my belly, blooming through my sex, dragging me under until it exploded my mind, my toes. "Zeus!" I cried. "Zeus!"

He didn't stop—he was building, building, fucking me,

breathless. Then he drove into me one last time, coming with a strangled yell.

He pressed his forehead to my forehead. His cock seemed to vibrate inside of me.

"Yes," I whispered, holding him tightly. "Yes."

He relaxed over me and groaned, panting.

"Yes," I whispered again.

He kissed me all over, then. He kissed my cheeks, my eyelids, my forehead, my hair. "Ice."

A little later, he pulled out of me and collapsed on my side, drawing me close. I held onto him and there we lay in the darkness, heating each other and not caring.

We said nothing for a long time. I listened to the distant buzzes and rumbles I'd been listening to for hours.

"Well," I joked. "What should we do now?"

He groaned and lifted himself up, pulled on my arm. "Come here." He moved toward the wall, and I fumbled after him. He sat himself back against the hot side of the container. I sat next to him, and he put his arm around me. "I don't want to pass out just yet."

"Pass out?"

"Lying there like that. It seems like we'd pass out sooner. I think—I'm not sure. Where's Thor when you need him, huh?"

I nestled closer. "Are you scared?"

"Not for me," he said. "Being pursued by these guys for so long, it's been a low-level tension for what feels like forever. Actually having it happen, it's a relief in a twisted way. I just don't want them to pull us out and torture us. Or really, torture you."

"You think that will happen?"

"At this point, no. It's been too long. Which makes me think that they have Odin and Thor, too."

"No!" My eyes stung.

"They would've come back by now if they didn't have them. They'd use our body parts to lure them."

The silence stretched long.

"I think it's over," he said. "I'm sorry. We should've gotten you home."

"I wanted to stay."

"Hey," he kissed my cheek. "I have a confession."

"What?"

"It's a big one, so get ready."

"Okay," I said.

"We didn't really take our names from gods."

"Huh?"

"Well, not really. They're from comic books."

I closed my eyes, smiling in the darkness as tears streamed from my eyes.

Oh, my badass Peter Pans.

"That is so..." *Sweet*, I thought, but it's not a thing you say to a man at a moment like this. "They're from comic books, but they're also from gods."

"I suppose you're right."

"I like that it's both."

I'm glad we got one of your comforters bought," he said. "I hope they don't lose the farm."

"Me, too," I said. "The other comforters were up with a longer lead time. I think they're getting lots of orders. I hope they're okay."

I felt a tear slide down my cheek.

"I bet they keep the farm. Your farm sounds nice. I can't believe you know how to make cheese and woolen goods and things. Were your folks hippies?"

"Kind of."

"It sounds amazing to make things like that. Simple things like that."

"Says the bank robber."

A long, dizzy silence. Then, "I wasn't always one. We weren't always robbers."

"What were you?"

"On the nothing chance we survive this, I shouldn't tell you." Zeus toyed with my hair.

I waited, hoping he'd say at least something.

"Screw it—I'll be vague," he said.

"I'm good with vague."

"We were...we're supposed to be dead, basically."

"Were you all in the military?"

"Good guess. Let's just say we were in intelligence," he said. "Odin and I were, not Thor. Thor was a doctor. He was overseas, working for an NGO—a volunteer medical organization. Thor saw something he shouldn't have, and he pursued it, tried to report it. He cracked open a massive can of worms. I'm not going to say where, but it was very huge, very damaging to certain people in power. Odin was sent to kill Thor. Odin got suspicious and didn't do the job. I was sent to kill Thor and Odin both."

"What did Thor see?"

"That's not important for this story. When I got there, I could see why Odin had hesitated. A few hours later, another guy was sent to kill all three of us."

"What happened to him?"

"Thor killed him. The guy had Odin and me down, and he didn't think Thor had it in him. Thor was up against a wall, this nerdy doctor. And the next thing we knew, Thor came out of nowhere and blew the man's head off."

He was silent for a while. His breathing sounded ragged.

"It fucked Thor up—you could see it. The horror in his eyes as he looked at the guy, lying there at his feet, half his head gone. And the three of us, we were suddenly dead men together. Targets on our back. It was literally us against the world. But it wasn't the world we were scared of—it was ZOX."

"ZOX?"

"They're big and bad and you don't want them after you," Zeus said.

"Because they do things like this."

"We went to Paris and got guest worker identities, and then went underground. We spent a few years in Rabat—in Morocco, where Odin's from. We got by. And we had help. Certain friends in intelligence. But the things we know make it so we'll always have guys on our trail, looking to kill us."

He sighed. He sounded so tired.

"We got good at knocking off banks as a ready source of cash. Turns out it takes a lot of cash to live under the radar. Odin's a very talented techie and psy-ops pro. I've got strategy. Thor has nerve. It made sense to come back to the States."

"You can't make a bargain? Where your secret goes public on your death? As an insurance policy so they won't kill you?"

"That stuff only works in the movies. People believe what they want to. Sometimes they believe pure bullshit, and sometimes they don't believe anything. It's better for them to have us dead and spin it."

"So you're not really robbers by choice. You're on the run."

"But we have each other. That's our family."

I rested my head on the metal wall, wondering what that felt like.

"You've been calming to Thor," Zeus added.

"You really don't think we can get out of this box, do you?"

"There's always a chance," Zeus said.

"Are you trying to get my hopes up?"

"Yup."

I smiled in the darkness. "You know that ruins it, right? When you tell the person you're trying to get her hopes up."

Zeus drew a finger down the side of my face. "Imagine being under a waterfall right now. You breathe in the sweet cool air, and cool water runs over you. And into your mouth."

He drew two fingers down the side of my hair. "Cool and sweet."

"Can I have a giant glass of lemonade, too?"

"While you're under the waterfall?"

"I'd like that very much, Zeus."

"You always want to have your cake and eat it too."

"Well?"

"Yes. A tall, icy, cool glass of lemonade to drink under the waterfall. In the cool air."

"Oh, that's nice." I rested my head on his shoulder. The heat felt oppressive, like it was pulsing in waves.

He tapped my cheek. "No sleeping."

"I wasn't sleeping."

"Yes, you were."

"Why not sleep?" I said. "Won't it be better?"

"I don't know," he said. "I've never been cooked like this. But I want you to stay awake," he said.

I snuggled close to him. "I want to stay awake."

We sat there breathing together, sweating together, cooking together, but not in the fun dinner party way.

My eyelids felt heavy. It felt good to close them, to let the darkness come.

Chapter Twenty-Three

I WOKE UP TO A BLINDING LIGHT.

I squinted and dark red shapes came into view. My eyeballs felt like they were coated with gravel. Not the best feeling.

"Hey, Ice! Isis!" Odin.

I groaned, turned, dimly aware of something falling off my forehead. A wet rag? Somebody put it back.

I grabbed at my arm, felt some kind of tubing in me.

"Leave it." Thor's voice. A hand clamped onto my wrist. "It's an IV. You need to get hydrated. Can you see me?"

I felt the bed next to me tip. Everything looked red. A finger was lifting my eyelid. A bright light flashed into one eye. The same on my other eye.

"Ugh!" I batted his hand away.

"Reaction time a little slow."

"Are you trying to insult me?" I mumbled.

A soft snicker. "Silliness intact."

"Where am I?"

"Motel. Not quite up to our usual standards, but bandits can't be choosers."

"Zeus?"

"Fine. We're all fine, Ice. We're safe."

"For now," Odin said.

I came around—slowly—over the next few hours. We were indeed in a motel, and Zeus was in the other bed.

"Thor says another two hours and your organs would've been putty," Odin said.

"That's nice," I mumbled. "So nice."

The next day was a blur of watching TV and being forced to drink a lot of unpleasant concoctions.

Thor and Odin had both been captured, it turned out. But the car they'd been put into was rammed—a drunk running a light, of all things.

It was a stroke of dumb luck, which Odin had managed to expertly exploit. He killed all but one of their captors, and Thor took over the wheel and sped from the scene of the accident.

Odin made the man tell where we were. Nobody would tell me exactly how he accomplished this.

I suppose I didn't want to know.

Another thing I didn't want to know was their plan for sending me back. The unsavory release-of-me-blindfolded-in-a-truck-stop plan had not been called off, though it had been delayed by our stint in the hot box.

We motel hopped over the next two days and landed in San Francisco on the third day. The big money from the robberies was lost, but we still had the diamonds, which Thor fenced downtown. After that, my bandits and I took up residence in one of the best hotels in the city. Another suite with another hot tub.

I felt well enough to eat a normal room service meal that night, but I was still a little weak. Zeus acted 100%, but I suspected he wasn't quite there yet, either.

Thor had instructed both Zeus and me to stay away from alcohol for the next few days. And no sex.

And no hot tubs.

Of course that didn't stop Odin and Thor from taking a long soak after dinner that night.

Zeus pulled the couch near the edge of the hot tub and we sat together, watching them float around in there, steam rising up.

As usual, we wore the hotel's special insignia robes. Lounging around all decadent in hotel robes was one of the gang's traditions, I was realizing. One of the things I'd miss when I had to leave.

"Being cooked isn't all it's cracked up to be," I said to Zeus.

"Agreed."

"We got through it, though," I reminded him hopefully. "It turned out great in the end."

He turned to me, as though reading my train of thought. "I can't let you stay," he said.

"We made an amazing team," I said.

"All the more reason for you to go home where you're safe," he said.

"How is that all the more reason?" I complained.

He lifted a gentle hand to my face and brushed a strand of hair off my forehead with a gaze so tender that my breath caught. "I thought you were going to die."

"I am going to die," I said. "We all are."

"We have to let you go. You all don't see it, but I do."

A shrill buzz pierced the lazy calm right then. Zeus shot up from the couch like an arrow. Odin and Thor were standing up in the hot tub, too, like they'd suddenly come to attention.

"What is it?" I asked.

"Phone," Thor said ominously.

Granted, it was a ringtone I'd never heard, but the way they were freaking out, you'd think a grizzly bear had smashed through the door.

Zeus went over to the side table where it had been charging and answered. "Yeah?"

He listened for a long time, expression dark. He thanked the person and set it down.

And looked right at me.

Shivers skittered down my spine. "What's wrong?"

"ZOX has a photo of you," he said. "They're trying to work out your identity."

"Our enemies? That ZOX?"

He nodded.

I stood, pulling my robe around me. "How'd they get a photo..."

"From a security camera on the fairgrounds."

Odin and Thor practically leapt out of the tub and started drying off.

"Oh my god," I said.

Odin sat down and fired up his laptop.

"What's going to happen?"

"Right now, the guys who are after us don't connect us with the Baylortown First City Bank job," Odin said. "That robbery's not even on their radar—they think we were somewhere else at the time."

"Thank goodness," Thor said.

"But they saw you with Zeus," Odin continued. "They stowed you in the shipping container with him. They know you're somebody to us. And now they have your picture."

"If they figure out who I am..." I clutched the robe more tightly, putting it all together.

"Not good," Zeus said. "It would not be good."

"My sisters!"

If ZOX figured out who I was, they would know about the farm. They could get to my sisters. They could threaten my sisters in an attempt to get leverage. Over me. Over my guys.

The thought of those ruthless people going after my sisters was too much. I felt like the whole world was about to crash down.

"Hey!" It was Thor, offering me juice.

I took the cool glass with numb fingers.

"Drink," he said.

I took a sip, letting the tangy liquid slide down my throat.

"Good." He took it from me. "Now breathe."

I sucked in a breath.

It didn't help.

Nothing would help now. We were screwed. Everybody I cared about was screwed. "They have a picture," I said. "And access to all the computers in the world. It's only a matter of time..."

"We're gonna figure it out," Zeus growled.

"How?"

"Because we will," Odin barked from where he tapped away at this laptop. "Because we're the biggest *fucking-g* badasses around, that's how."

I nodded, wanting desperately to believe them. But even the biggest badasses in the world couldn't turn back time.

Or could they?

~ The End ~

DANGEROUS ROYALS

Dark and edgy mafia romance; read in order

Dark Mafia Prince

Wicked Mafia Prince

Savage Mafia Prince

Annika Martin writes in many genres; find a complete list of her books, audiobooks, and translated works at www.annikamartinbooks.com

All the Annika deets!

Annika Martin is a New York Times bestselling author who lives in Minneapolis with her non-bank-robber husband. In her spare time she enjoys taking pictures of her cats, consuming boatloads of chocolate suckers, and tending her wild, bee-friendly garden.

newsletter:
http://annikamartinbooks.com/newletter

TikTok:
@annikamartinauthor

Facebook:
www.facebook.com/AnnikaMartinBooks

Instagram:
instagram.com/annikamartinauthor

website:
www.annikamartinbooks.com

Reader group of awesomeness
www.facebook.com/groups/AnnikaMartinFabulousGang/